the *Life* of *Glass*

Also by Jillian Cantor

The September Sisters

the *Life* of *Glass*

JILLIAN CANTOR

An Imprint of HarperCollinsPublishers

HarperTeen is an imprint of HarperCollins Publishers.

The Life of Glass

Library of Congress Cataloging-in-Publication Data
Cantor, Jillian.
      The life of glass / Jillian Cantor. — 1st ed.
            p.   cm.
      "HarperTeen."
      Summary: Through her freshman year of high school, fourteen-year-old Melissa
struggles to hold on to memories of her deceased father, to cope with her mother's return
to dating, to get along with her sister, and to sort out her feelings about her best friend,
Ryan.
      ISBN 978-0-06-168651-1
      [1. Interpersonal relations—Fiction.   2. Death—Fiction.   3. High schools—
Fiction.   4. Schools—Fiction.   5. Single-parent families—Fiction.   6. Family
life—Southwest, New—Fiction.   7. Southwest, New—Fiction.]   I. Title.
PZ7.C173554Lif   2010   2009001758
[Fic]—dc22   CIP
                                                                                        AC

Typography by Amy Toth
10   11   12   13   14   CG/RRDB   10   9   8   7   6   5   4   3   2   1
❖
First Edition

For Gregg—who always makes me feel beautiful

chapter *1*

The last thing my father ever told me was that it takes glass a million years to decay. I knew it was true because my father always knew things like that, strange sorts of things that no one else cared to remember or learn in the first place. Before he got sick, he was writing a book called *Strange Love*, which apparently referenced some song he and my mother had loved in the eighties, and also the fact that the book was all about his obsession with bizarre tidbits of information and unusual love stories. He'd only written two chapters when he was diagnosed with lung cancer, but he had a journal full of notes already waiting.

My father had never smoked a day in his life, so there was a strange fact just wrapped up in his diagnosis. It was something that made him laugh, an odd sort of laugh, a short snarl that reminded me of an angry dog and only stopped when my mother started sobbing quietly into her hands. My sister, Ashley, and I had shared a plastic chair in the back corner of Dr. Singh's office, our bare summer legs touching. It was cold enough in there that we both had goose bumps. This was four years ago, when I was only ten and Ashley was twelve, and it was the first time I'd ever seen my mother cry, so I knew something terrible was about to happen.

By the time he told me the fact about the glass, it was two and a half years later. He was lying under a blue wool blanket in a hospice bed in our living room. He had a morphine drip in his arm and a short, raspy tone to his voice. He looked small and old enough to have been the same age as my grandpa Jack, who died when he was seventy-seven. My father was forty-one.

He'd spent two months before that night in his hospice bed, so it was something I'd gotten used to seeing when I walked in after school, something I had to navigate my way around if I wanted to get to the couch to watch television. I read a lot in my room those two months. Some nights after dinner, my mother rapped on the door, poked her head in, and said, "Melissa, why don't you keep your father company?"

I'd lie and say I had a lot of homework even if I didn't. And she'd frown and get this sort of stern, perplexed look on her face, so her brow would get real tight. My mother is beautiful, and she hates frowning. She's tall and thin with silky raven hair and smooth, pale skin. When I was younger and I first watched *Snow White*, I thought the character had been modeled after my mother, as if she were an amazing creation good enough for Disney. But she always told me that beauty was something you had to work for, and work she did—filing and polishing and loofah-ing and moisturizing—all the stuff I wasn't that interested in, no matter how hard she and Ashley tried.

After my mother left my room, I'd close the door, open the window, climb out, and drop to the ground. It was a wonderfully freeing feeling, my feet hitting the crushed rock below my window. If my mother had been really smart or really paying attention to me she would've thought to install the prickly pear cactus right below my bedroom window when she'd redone the landscaping the summer before. But my mother had no idea that I went out at night, that the window was my escape route.

I'd leave my bike parked by the side of my house, and I'd get on it and ride down the night street until I got to Ryan's house, which was only six houses down from mine. Ryan's father is a Border Patrol agent, and he works a lot at night, leaving Ryan home alone. If his father's car wasn't in the driveway, I'd knock on the door, but if it was, I'd throw little rocks at Ryan's window until he opened it up. If his father was already asleep, he'd climb out and hop on his bike, and then we'd ride wildly out in the night, into the open desert behind our street.

There is a large wash, an empty dry riverbed, that runs behind our development. It's far enough back so people can't see us but close enough to hop on our bikes and ride. And ride we did, through the wash, in the prickly dark desert night, the heat or the cool, depending on the season, enveloping us in a dry, crisp blanket. During the monsoon storms of summer, the wash fills up with water and becomes a raging river, cutting up the developments in the area for a few days until the dry air charges back in and dries it up again. Most of the time the wash is empty, long, and dark. The perfect place to ride bikes, to explore, to get lost.

"Let's race," Ryan would say, and we'd go on our bikes, legs pumping, breath exploding out of our chests, all the way down the wash until we hit the railroad tracks, nearly four miles, a distance I'd once walked with my father.

And that night, the last night I ever talked to my father, the moon was full and hung bright and heavy in the clear April sky. The air was pleasant and achingly dry, though I knew that soon it would be summer, that the heat would become unbearable, the moon swallowed whole by thick monsoon clouds, the wash consumed with water. And it occurred to me, as I was riding my bike, that I hoped my father would die before then. School would be out in another month, and the thought of having to sit home all alone in the house, having to avoid him or talk to him was unbearable. It was a terrible thing to think, and I hated myself for it.

"Hey, Mel, look at this." Ryan had stopped, and he was shining his flashlight off to the side of the wash.

"What?" I got off my bike and went to him. He held an object, an artifact, in his hand. "What is it?"

"I dunno." He shined the light directly on it. It was small enough to fit in his palm and could've been a seashell, except it was made out of rainbow glass, all the different colors reaching and swirling in the light. People left strange things in the wash, and other things were swept in with the rain and wind: trash and treasure, beer bottles, old tire scraps, jewelry. Once my father had found half a diamond tennis bracelet, strewn across a heap of sagebrush.

"Here," Ryan said. "Take it."

"Why?" But I held my hand out and took it. The glass felt cold and smooth.

He grinned, and the metal of his braces gleamed off the flashlight. "A souvenir." Ryan was shorter than I was and a little too skinny. We'd been friends since we were seven, when he and his father moved into the neighborhood from Dallas, after his mother had left them both for the guy who'd mowed their lawn. Ryan said that was part of the reason his father liked living in the desert—no lawns—but I didn't really see what the point was anyway, if she was already gone.

Ryan was quiet at school, in that he didn't really have any friends but me and one other guy, Todd Tremaine. But when his asthma got bad, I could hear him breathing, even from across the classroom—a sound that sometimes reassured me, just a little bit.

When my father first got sick, my family left to go to Philadelphia for three months so my father could try an experimental treatment, Ryan took notes for me, and he emailed me all my homework so I didn't get behind. My supposed best friend since kindergarten, Kelly Jamison, didn't even send me a single email the whole time I was gone, and when I came back, she gave me half a smile and a wave. And that was when Ryan became my best friend, when I learned the number of pedal strokes between his house and mine (thirty-six).

I had other souvenirs from the wash. On school breaks or weekends, Ryan and I would sometimes walk back there together, scavenging for something. Our best find yet: a thin green street sign that read STREET ROAD. Ryan hung it in his room and then lied to his father and told him I'd brought it back for him as a present from Philadelphia.

So on that particular night, I took the piece of glass, smooth and hard and colorful, and placed it in the pocket of my jeans.

When I snuck back into my house, I came in through the front door. My mother was a sound sleeper; she popped Lunesta like candy. Ashley was in her room at the other end of the house, probably lying in her bed with her headphones on, and my father—well, I didn't imagine he would hear me.

As I closed the door behind me, I heard the buzz

from one of his machines; then I heard a whisper, like a ghost at first. "Cynthia." He called out for my mom again. "Cyn?" I thought about keeping quiet, tiptoeing off to my room, my mother never the wiser, but I couldn't do it.

"No, Dad, it's me."

"Melon?"

"Yeah?" I walked toward him, promising myself I wouldn't look, that if I didn't see him I could pretend his voice was just groggy, thick with sleep and half-forgotten dreams.

"What do you have there?" I had taken the glass out of my pocket and was fingering it nervously in my hand.

"Nothing. Just something I found."

"In the wash?"

"Yeah." I didn't see the point of lying to him.

"Melon—"

"You won't tell Mom?"

"Let me see it." My father loved artifacts almost as much as he loved facts. He might've been an archaeologist in some other lifetime if he hadn't been an accountant with Charles and Large.

I switched on the table lamp, sat at the edge of the

couch, and showed it to him. And that's when he said it, when he told me that if I'd left it lying there in the wash, it would've taken this glass a million years to decay.

"A million years," I mused. It was amazing, the way humans were just flesh and bones, and so susceptible to being broken down into so much less than that, into shadows and old men and hospice-bed figures, and yet glass could stay whole for so long.

That night I sat there and waited for him to say something else, but I only heard his breathing, so shallow and raspy that I couldn't be sure it was there at all.

The next morning, my dad's nurse, Annette, came at 7 A.M. as always, and I heard her, as I walked from my room to the hallway bathroom, my head thick and dulled with sleep. "Now he's at peace, Mrs. Cynthia," she said to my mother.

"I can't believe he's actually gone," my mother said. Her voice sounded lower than usual, and scratchy with what I assumed to be tears.

I sat there and soaked the news in, filled with this odd sense of regret, relief, terror.

Ashley came out of her room, her hair in twisty rollers, white pimple cream dotted on her chin. In an hour her curls would splash against her shoulders, her skin would look flawless and smooth underneath her foundation. "What's going on?" she asked. I shrugged. "Well, why are you standing in the middle of the hallway?"

"I'm not," I lied. I wasn't going to be the one to tell her.

"Melissa." Our eyes met for a second, and I saw it in there, that she knew, that we both knew. There would be no more tomorrows and cluttered living rooms and things divided in fours. "Mom," she yelled. "Mom."

My mother ran into the hallway. Her hair was back in a ponytail and she wasn't wearing any makeup, but she still looked beautiful. Her eyes flickered, so she looked up, then down, then straight at Ashley. "I'm sorry," she said. "Annette said he went peacefully. In his sleep."

It was so expected and terrible and normal and almost a little bit like a release, and the three of us just stood there looking at one another. There was nothing to say. Nowhere else to go. Until finally I said, "Are we going to school today?"

"Melissa!" Ashley turned and ran back to her room.

"No." My mother sighed. "No, I suppose you don't have to. Unless you want to."

I nodded. I did want to go. I didn't want to see what might happen next. Didn't want to know how my father might leave our house for the last time, what might happen to the hospice bed, the equipment, or listen from the other room as my mother made the calls I knew she was bound to make.

I went back to my room and threw on some jeans and a shirt, and then I picked up the piece of glass from the wash and put it in my pocket. And even now I sometimes carry it with me, as if it were some kind of good-luck charm, the last thing of mine my father ever touched.

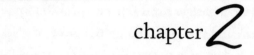

chapter 2

At first the time without my father came in minutes. I watched them tick by on my watch the morning he died. They came slowly, all through pre-algebra, earth science, advanced English, social studies, and PE.

Then I watched it turn into hours. Days. Weeks. Months.

My first day of high school was exactly one year, two months, and three weeks after he died. And by then, most of the physical remnants of him had disappeared from my life. My mother kept only one thing that I could tell: the portrait that hung in our front hallway that we'd gotten done at Sears when I was five and Ashley was seven. My father looked so young in that picture, and he had a beard, something that must have been a fad that year, because I can't remember him ever having a beard except for in that picture.

The one thing I had was his journal of facts and stories, the notes he'd been taking for his book. I'd taken them out of the computer room the afternoon after he'd died, before my mother could decide to throw them out.

In the past year I'd mulled them over, committing some to memory. I read the pages slowly, one a week, so that every seven days I had something new, another gift from my father. I could imagine him telling me the fact or a story with a chuckle, or a smile, or a pursed upper lip.

After I got dressed for my first day of high school, I flipped through the pages, looking for something interesting, some tidbit that could tide me through the day or fill me up with a new and necessary knowledge.

This is what I found: It is impossible to cry in space, without gravity. So I wondered if it was possible to be sad there. If there was sadness without tears.

I heard my father's voice: "Imagine that, Melon. That your body would respond one way, and the world would just reject it."

◇

Desert Crest High School was about a half mile from our house, double the distance of the middle school, and at the top of a long, steep hill. Ryan and I had been riding our bikes to school together since the beginning of seventh grade, and when I went outside on the first morning of high school he was already waiting for me in the street.

"Hey, Mel." He waved. "Ready for the big time?" He was always saying odd, dorky things that sounded like they'd come out of the mouth of someone's grand-father.

I laughed. "Yeah, whatever." The truth was, I was a little nervous. It was the first time Ashley and I would be in the same school together since elementary school, and I knew she'd been dreading it. She'd been complaining about it to our mom all week. "Don't expect me to act like I know you or anything," she'd sneered to me at the dinner table the night before.

Ashley had gotten her driver's license over the sum-mer, after which she'd taken my father's Camry. It didn't seem right, that she'd claimed it as her own, and I wished my mother had sold it or donated it along with every-thing else.

Now that Ashley had it, the inside smelled like

bubblegum and pineapple perfume, all the smells of him obliterated. I used to love driving in his car with him because it always smelled so dark and rich, like fresh-brewed coffee.

As I hopped on my bike, Ashley zipped out of the driveway and sped by in the Camry, failing to stop completely at the stop sign up ahead. I imagined that inside the car she was checking her lip gloss in the rearview mirror.

"She could at least offer us a ride," Ryan complained as we started pedaling. In mid-August the air was still heavy with monsoon moisture and crushing heat. I felt sweat instantly beading up on my brow, and I could hear Ryan's heavy breath as we began to pedal hard up the hill. I wondered what would happen if he stopped breathing, if he just ceased to be. The possibility terrified me, sank into my chest, hard and terrible like a rock.

"We don't want to go with her anyway."

"We don't?"

"She has to go pick up Mr. September."

Ryan rolled his eyes. Austin White was Ashley's very new boyfriend and also the cocaptain of the baseball team. Ryan and I were betting they'd be broken up by the end of September, which is how Ryan had thought of the nickname. He said it was even funnier if you knew anything about baseball (which I didn't), because there was some famous player who was called Mr. October.

Austin was supposedly very good, and Ashley had taken a new interest in baseball. She'd sit there in front of the TV at night, squinting at the plays. "Well, what does that mean?"

My mother would shake her head. "Oh, who cares?" she'd say. "Ashley, what's gotten into you? This, over some boy?"

"He's not just some boy, Mom." Her eyes got this sort of dreamy, faraway sheen to them, but I didn't think it was love. Austin was tall and muscular with blond hair and a tanned face, and I thought Ashley was counting on the fact that they'd still be dating in the spring and then she would have a chance at being crowned queen of the spring formal.

"You should tell your mom," Ryan said. He knew about my mother's rule that Ashley was not allowed to drive anyone else except for me.

I shrugged. "It's not worth it." I thought about what Ashley had said the night before, that she wasn't going to admit to knowing me. And the truth was, I'd rather be riding my bike, sweating with Ryan, than sitting in the cool, uncomfortable silence of the car with her.

The high school was much larger than our middle school and strangely menacing. You had to walk up a wide row of cement steps to even get into the school. I counted them the first time up. Twenty. Twenty long steps that led to a seemingly ominous set of double doors. People rushed past, bumping into us as if they didn't even see us, calling out to friends, hugging each other, screaming. I thought about my dad's fact, that without gravity there were no tears, that emotion itself became void, and I wondered if that could be true in a place like this too, a place that was large enough to swallow you whole without anybody even noticing.

The school was so big that it was a challenge just to find where my classes were. I had Algebra 2 first, then social studies. Third period, just before lunch, I had biology, and when I walked into the room, I was thrilled to see Ryan already sitting there.

He got a big, goofy grin on his face when he saw me, and I slid into the seat next to him.

"Thank God," I whispered.

On the downside, our teacher, Mr. Finkelstein, talked

in a monotone and droned on and on about how we were going to have to dissect things, starting with a frog first semester and a pig in the spring. "Cool," Ryan whispered to me. I made a face at him.

After lunch I had Spanish with a crotchety old lady who refused to speak a word of English, even on the first day, so I had no idea what she was saying, and then I had PE with a very manly looking woman who seemed really into field hockey. Ugh.

Last period was advanced English, and I could tell I was going to like it right away. My teacher, Mrs. Connor, seemed really cool. She was short, with a high, dramatic voice and little spectacles, and I felt a little like I was watching some sort of theater production when she stood in front of the class, because she was so lively and jumped around a lot. "Poetry is a shadow," she yelled out to us. She wore this big red floppy hat with a feather in it, something that made her look like some movie star from the 1940s. I loved her inherent kookiness, something I was sure my father would've appreciated, a story for his book.

On the bike ride home, Ryan untucked his shirt as we rode, and he laughed wildly. "Freedom," he yelled to me. "Ahh, freedom."

I laughed. But I imagined how the days were going to drag on and on and on, and how long it would be until we got a break again.

I also felt a little disappointed, because in my head I'd been imagining high school to be this grand, glorious place with tons of new and interesting people. But in reality, it seemed just like junior high, only big enough that now I was invisible.

"I'll race you to the wash," Ryan called out as he sped up to pass me.

I stood up to gain some speed, and even though sweat was falling into my eyes, I pedaled harder to catch him.

At the beginning of the second week, Mr. Finkelstein pushed us right into things by dropping the plastic bags containing the dead frogs on our lab tables. "Take good care of him," he told us all as he stood in front of the room and wrung his hands together. "He's your one and only."

I made a face at Ryan. It was weird and creepy that this guy was telling us to take care of something that was already dead and that we were planning on mutilating, which dropped biology into my second-worst class, just ahead of PE and possibly tied with Spanish.

Luckily, we got to pick our lab partners, so Ryan and I paired up, and he said he didn't mind wielding the scalpel. "Come here, little guy." Ryan rolled him over in the tray almost tenderly before making the first cut.

"Don't talk to him like that," I said.

"Like what?"

"I don't know, like he's your pet or something."

Ryan shrugged. "He needs a name." He held up the frog so the dead little face was staring at me. I turned away.

"How about Kermit?" Not entirely creative but the first thing that popped into my head for a frog.

He laughed. "Then in the spring we'll have Miss Piggy."

"Or Mr. Piggy, depending on what we get."

"Okay, Kermit," Ryan said. "Sorry about this." He held up the scalpel; I didn't watch as he made the first cut.

The day after we started on the frog, a new girl joined us in bio. "Class," Mr. Finkelstein droned. I looked up, the world blurry and swimming through my lab goggles. "Let's all welcome Courtney Whitman, shall we?"

We all mumbled hi and turned our attention back to our frogs. And to tell you the truth, I didn't pay too much attention to her at first.

chapter 3

Before my father died, my mother hadn't worked. For a few weeks after his death, my mother spent nights sitting at the kitchen table poring over all the bills. There was a bill for some huge sum of money from the agency that had sent us Annette, which my mother grumbled about not being able to pay. I suddenly wondered how we were going to live, where we were going to get money. "Are we going to move?" I asked her.

She sighed. "Why would you say that, Melissa?"

"I don't know." I was thinking about Jessica Snyder, who'd been my good friend in fourth grade. Her father had lost his job, and then three months later they'd moved out of their house to go live with her aunt in Phoenix. We only had my grandma Harry, who had been in an assisted-living facility and had recently moved into the nursing-home part because her Alzheimer's was getting worse. My mother's sister, Julie, lived with her husband in Pennsylvania. They were both sort of stuffy sociology professors, and I knew it was cold there, so I hoped we weren't going to go live with her.

"I don't know what we're going to do, sweetie. This wasn't in my plan, you know." She laughed, but it was a high-pitched kind of laugh that sounded like it could turn into crying at any moment. "You just don't plan for this. Not really." She paused. "We'll get the life-insurance money, but that will only go so far. And I haven't had a job since your sister was born, in well, my God, that's been nearly sixteen years." She stood up and walked toward the sliding glass door that led out to our tiny backyard, which was filled with crushed rock, cacti, and a small irrigated square of grass. "Where does the time go anyway?" she mused.

Usually my mother had perfect posture and a wide smile that showed off her completely straight, white, tiny teeth. I had what my mother called horse teeth, big and square, inherited from my father's side of the family. So I always tried to smile with my mouth closed.

She walked away from the door, and she smoothed back my hair. "Don't you worry, sweetie. I'll get it all figured out."

My mother had been a teenage beauty queen. Or I guess the truth was she'd been first runner-up in a lot of beauty pageants, but she won one. She was Queen of the Rodeo in 1986. She has the picture of herself, sitting proud atop a horse, her long black hair flowing past her shoulders, a sparkly tiara on her head, and a sash over a pink dress. The picture is hanging in her bedroom, right next to her dresser.

She told us once that right before they took that picture the horse tried to throw her, and she ended up falling in the dirt. "But did I cry?" She shook her head. "No, girls. I brushed myself off and got right back on that horse, and see, look here, you wouldn't even know it, would you?"

The day after my mother and I had our talk, she went out and got a job washing hair at a salon. After a few weeks she decided to go to beauty school and get her degree.

When she was in beauty school, she always wanted to practice on Ashley and me. I was the guinea pig, the one she experimented on when she didn't know what she was doing yet, not really, anyway. I hated having her tug at my hair, having her cut it into some new style. I didn't like seeing a new person when I looked in the mirror, seeing the unfamiliar shape of my face, with slightly uneven shorter layers. My cheeks were too fat and my nose a little too big. I had the same jet-black hair as my mother and Ashley, but while theirs was straight and shiny, mine had a little bit of a frizzy wave to it.

After one terrible, oddly layered cut, I refused to help her out. "Oh, come on, Melissa," my mother would say, tugging at the ends of my crooked hair. "Let me fix it up."

I shook my head. "It's fine. Just leave it."

Ashley rolled her eyes. "She doesn't even care about her hair. Seriously, Melissa. Someday, you'll grow up and want to look pretty."

Just before I started high school, my mother got a job as an assistant stylist at a salon called Belleza, which she told me meant "beauty" in some other language. It was a very upscale place, and the people who went there had money, which my mother said meant she would get really good tips.

But now, for the first time, the house was empty after

school. My mother didn't get home until around seven, when she'd stumble in wearing her black dress and heels, pop some frozen dinners in the microwave, and sit down on the couch and rub her ankles.

Usually Ashley would drive Mr. September home after baseball practice (I'd heard a rumor that he'd crashed his own car over the summer and his parents hadn't gotten him a new one yet). She'd hang out with him at his house for a while, since both his parents worked late and, as she'd mentioned, giving me a snide look, he didn't have a younger sister. As if it were my fault that I had nowhere else to go.

But I was glad she didn't bring him here. I'd walked by the two of them at school a few times. Austin would have Ashley pinned against his locker, and they'd be kissing so furiously that it looked like he was about to suck her face off. I couldn't imagine that that was really love.

If Ryan's father was at work, he'd come over and hang out with me, which was the same thing we'd done in junior high school too, only then my mom had been home most of the time, and she'd brought us snacks of fresh-baked cookies and apple slices. Now, as we lay on the floor of the den and watched TV, we had only stale potato chips to munch on.

Ryan had grown taller than me over the summer, and as we stretched out on the floor, tumbling over couch pillows, I'd been noticing how long his legs were getting, how it seemed possible he could outgrow the room, that he would all at once be too big to hang out on the floor with me.

But when he started to cough and wheeze, and he pulled his inhaler out of his shorts pocket and sucked on it in one rapid puff, he was also still that little boy from down the street.

One afternoon in the beginning of September, as we were sitting there on the floor in the den watching some lady scream obscenities at the man who may or may not have been the father of her child, Ryan suddenly said, "What do you think about Courtney?"

"Courtney?" I thought he was talking about the lady on TV at first, and I hadn't known her name was Courtney, so I was thinking, wow, he must really be paying attention to this garbage, whereas I was more zoning out and decompressing from a long day.

"You know, Courtney Whitman. From biology."

Yes, then I did know. In the few weeks since she'd joined our class, I'd heard that Courtney Whitman had just moved to our school from San Diego, and she was what my father would've called a total Valley Girl. Long blond hair and perky blue eyes and tall and tanned and really big-chested. I was still struggling to fill out my A cup. My mother said I was either just a late bloomer in this department or I took after my grandma Harry, who always had really small boobs. "She's okay," I said. "Why?"

"I dunno." He shrugged.

I nudged him. "You like her?" His face turned bright red, and he stuffed a handful of chips in his mouth. Then he shrugged. "You do like her."

"Just forget it," he said. "Forget I ever said anything." But I couldn't. Because Ryan didn't like girls like Courtney Whitman, and Courtney Whitman didn't like guys like Ryan. Or did she? I took a good hard look at him. Straight white teeth (now that the braces were gone), tall, lanky and tan, sandy blond hair that he gelled up just a little bit. "Hey," he finally said, and I realized I'd been staring just a little too closely. "Wanna go ride in the wash? My dad has to work late."

I nodded. "Yeah, whatever. Let's go."

I got back around five, and the house was still quiet. Ashley usually paraded in about thirty minutes before my mother. She didn't tell my mom that she spent that much time with Austin, and I didn't either. Though we both knew I could hold it over her head if there was something I really wanted from her.

I sat on the couch and watched TV by myself for a while, flipping channels through various boring news reports. Then I went upstairs to my room and decided I would flip through my dad's journal to try to find something to pick me up. I had to read through a few pages of my dad's messy, sprawling handwriting until I found something that made me laugh. "The longest recorded flight of the chicken: 13 seconds." I tried to imagine the chicken, squawking and squealing as it tried to make it off the ground, and then I thought about the poor sap who actually went out with the stopwatch and tried to record the thing, and for some reason that made me giggle.

My mom was in a good mood when she came home. I heard her singing to herself. "Did you have a good day, sweetie?" She blew me an air kiss.

"Yeah. It was fine."

"Where's your sister?"

I shrugged. "Probably in her room." I hadn't heard

her come in, but it's not like she announced herself when she did.

"Well, go see if you can find her. I want to talk to you girls."

I do not like that line. I remembered when my father had said it, just before we left for Philadelphia. *I want to talk to you girls. We're going to take a trip east for a while, a few months.* That was when I knew he was really, really sick, that it was more serious than he'd let on.

"Ashley," I called down the hallway. "Mom's home."

She opened her bedroom door. She had the phone up to her ear, and she pointed at it as if to say, *Shut up, can't you see I'm doing something?*

"She wants to talk to us," I said, enunciating each word carefully as if I were talking to some sort of idiot.

Ashley sighed, long and deep and melodramatic. I rolled my eyes. "I have to call you back," she said. "The imp is here." The imp. That's what she called me to her friends. I hated when she called me that, though I never would let her know that it bothered me. I thought it made me sound incredibly small and incredibly ugly.

I walked back toward the kitchen without her. "She's coming," I said to my mom as I plopped down at the table. "What's for dinner?"

"Oh, I don't know, sweetie. I hadn't really thought about it yet." She opened the freezer door. "There's still some Swansons left."

"Okay," I said, though I had become seriously sick of salty, frozen fried chicken and mashed potatoes. But I didn't have it in me to make her feel bad about it.

Ashley walked in and sat in the seat next to me. "Hi, sweetie," my mom said. Ashley smiled sweetly at her, then turned and made a face at me when my mother turned around to shut the freezer door.

"That is so not attractive," I whispered to her, wondering how Mr. September would feel about her if he saw her like that, her tiny little features all scrunched up like a rabbit. Not so kissable now.

"Look who's talking. Nice hair." I'd put my hair up in a ponytail when I was riding my bike, and I could tell that wisps had flown out everywhere, all the layers still a little uneven from when my mom had practiced on me. I reached up to try to smooth it out.

"Now, girls," my mother was saying, "I have something I need to tell you."

"Spill," Ashley said. "I have to call Austin back in ten minutes."

I rolled my eyes, though neither one of them was looking at me.

"I don't quite know how to say this." She looked at me. Then at Ashley. Then back at me.

I felt this terrible knot in my stomach, an ache rising up through my esophagus and dying to come out of my throat, a loud wail, a horrible howling scream. She had cancer. She was sick. She was going to die. Finally Ashley said, "Well?"

"Well, girls. I've met someone." The words washed over me, spilled into my brain like the enormous wave I'd just been surfing on had exploded all around me, trapping me inside tons and tons of rushing water so I couldn't hear or speak or breathe. "It's nothing serious, mind you. But I'm going to go on a date with him. Just a dinner really. I don't even know if you would call it a date."

"Okay," Ashley said, all nonchalantly like our mother just decided to go on a date every day of the week and it was no big deal. "Can I go call Austin now?"

"I thought maybe we could talk about it. If you girls wanted to." She was looking right at me when she said it, and I looked away.

"Whatever," Ashley said. "I'll help you find something to wear if you want."

My mother smiled at her, reached over for her hand, and squeezed it. "Thanks, sweetie. I'd like that a lot." She paused and I could feel her eyes on me. "Melissa . . ."

"What?" I shrugged.

"You're awfully quiet."

I wanted to tell her that I didn't think it was right that she was dating someone, anyone. But I knew she and Ashley would gang up on me and try to convince me it was great, the way they did about everything else. The two of them were always like best friends, and I was the odd woman out. So instead I said, "Well, why would I care what you do? You're an adult."

"Really, sweetie? You mean that? You're being very mature about this. . . ."

I nodded. I wanted to know who this man was, where she met him, why she wanted to go to dinner with him. I always thought that there was one person you were supposed to love, and that once you used up your love with this person or it got thrown away or wasted or whatever, you were done. It had never occurred to me before that my mother was going to look for that love all over again. "I think I'm going to go start my homework," I said.

"What about dinner?"

"I'm not that hungry anymore."

She sighed, and I knew she understood what I really meant, that I was not being mature, that I was not okay with it. I felt sick to my stomach, a terrible burning at the core of me. Maybe it was an ulcer. Maybe it would start to bleed, and I would go in my room and close my eyes for the night and never wake up. And then my mother and Ashley would be their own happy little family, all beauty pageants and body glitter.

In my room, I didn't look at my homework. I took out my seashell piece of glass and ran my fingers against it.

It was crazy the way I could break this glass, shatter it so quickly with just one false move, but I could not kill it, not really, not for a million years. Whereas it was so hard for people to break, but we could get sick or die in what seemed like a matter of seconds.

chapter 4

A few days later, in biology, I caught Ryan stealing glances at Courtney Whitman. She and her lab partner were assigned to the table next to ours, and as luck would have it, her partner was out for the day.

We were all looking pretty stupid in our safety goggles and rubber gloves, picking through this poor dead frog carcass with tweezers. I had yet to identify anything; all the innards looked oddly the same to me, so it was Ryan who was doing most of the work and pointing things out to me. He didn't mind because I'd promised to help him out with his English papers.

So Ryan was picking through Kermit, cutting for the

heart, our assignment for the day: find the organ, identify it, draw it in our workbook. I watched him look up
every so often to gawk at Courtney, and as I was watching him watch her, I got this sick feeling in my stomach.
Maybe she felt his eyes on her, or maybe she was just
seriously lost without her partner, but she looked up and
said, "Can I work with you guys today?"

Ryan looked as if he'd just swallowed his tongue. So
I finally said, "Yeah. Sure, whatever."

Mr. Finkelstein had paired her up with the odd man
out, the only one of us not to have a partner, Jeffrey Gib-
son. Jeffrey was absolutely the nerdiest kid in our grade,
if not the whole entire school. He had really thick horn-
rimmed glasses and wore his pants up too high, and he
played the flute in the marching band, and he was really,
really into the whole band thing, so even when you saw
him just walking down the hallway he was doing that
funny rolling step that the band kids did on the field. But
he was also incredibly good at science, and I had no doubt
that he was the one doing all the work on the frog.

So Courtney picked up her frog tray and moved it on
over to our table. Ryan seemed to be concentrating very
hard on Kermit suddenly, and Courtney leaned over his
shoulder. "You have such a steady hand," she practically

cooed into his ear, so I had to roll my eyes. "Wow." She popped her gum, which we were not supposed to be chewing in the biology lab, and I looked around to see if Mr. Finkelstein had noticed. Nope. He sat behind his desk absorbed in a stack of papers, and I wondered what he was thinking about. Probably not us. "You're so lucky, Melinda, to have such a cool partner."

"Melissa," I corrected her.

"Oh. Melissa. I'm sorry. It sucks being new." She frowned, and for a moment, I felt bad for her. I remembered what it was like to come back to school after a marking period in Philadelphia and an entire summer, and even though I knew most of the kids, everyone was new and different and everything had changed. But it was hard to really sympathize with someone so beautiful and perfect-looking—and you could still tell, even with the goggles wrapped around her head. Her shiny blond hair hit her shoulders perfectly. Her blue eyeliner and blue eyes only seemed bluer with the goggles. "And you're Ryan, right?"

He looked up from the frog and pushed the goggles up his nose. "I am." He smiled at her. They kind of stared at each other for a minute or two and I started to feel really uncomfortable, as if I were interrupting something, which was crazy because she was at my lab table with my lab partner. "Here," he said, and reached for her tray. "Let me find it for you."

"Oh." She giggled and shot me a smile. "Thank you."

Ryan cut with perfect precision, as if our frog had only been practice, and with Courtney's frog he was an expert with the skills of a surgeon. "Here you go," he said after a few minutes. "Your heart."

"Thank you, thank you. I never could've found it on my own," she said. He nodded, red spreading across his cheeks from underneath his goggles. "Hey, Meliss, want to trade partners?" She laughed.

I glared at her. "No thanks."

"Just kidding," she said. But Ryan was silent, and the notion that he would trade me away made me feel as if I were about to puke.

I was still annoyed with Ryan after school, so I didn't wait for him to ride home together like I normally did.

"Hey, Mel, wait up." I heard him call after me, but I didn't stop pedaling. I pedaled hard and furious, my legs pumping, a hot breeze cutting through my hair.

It took him a few blocks to catch up. I heard his heavy

breathing behind me, and then I slowed down, afraid that he was going to have an asthma attack. "What's your problem?" he asked.

I shrugged. "I just didn't feel like waiting. Okay? I have stuff to do."

"Like what stuff?"

"I don't know. Stuff, all right? Jeez. We don't always have to ride together." I was waiting for him to tell me I was wrong, that we did need to ride together, that I meant something.

But all he said was, "Yeah, all right. I get it."

We got to my house and we both stopped. He was still breathing hard, the breath catching in his chest in that thick, raspy asthmatic way that was so familiar that I'd become used to it over the past few years. I felt a little bad that I'd made him ride so hard. "You wanna come in?" I asked. "Or ride in the wash?"

"Nah." He shook his head. "I shouldn't. My dad's home."

I watched him turn and ride down the street toward his house before I went inside.

The Saturday morning of my mother's date, I convinced Ashley to drive me to the nursing home to visit Grandma

Harry. Well, not so much convinced really, but blackmailed by threatening to tell my mother that she'd been driving Mr. September to school. She glared at me, but she grabbed the car keys and started walking toward the garage, so I followed.

Truthfully, I could've ridden my bike. It was only three miles to the home, but the day was hot and the late-morning sun was bright and biting, and I didn't feel like arriving red-faced and sweating to see her.

Ashley didn't say a word to me the whole ride over there, and when we got there, she didn't even park. She pulled up, right in front of the Sunset Vistas sign, a name that always struck me as odd because it sounded more like a resort than a hospital for old people. "I'll be back in twenty minutes," she said.

"Don't you want to come in with me?" I knew she wouldn't. Ashley hated visiting Grandma Harry since her memory got so bad. She said it was too depressing to watch, so she basically ignored her unless my mother made her go visit on Mother's Day or Grandma Harry's birthday.

"Be waiting outside or I'm leaving without you," she said. I got out of the car and barely slammed the door shut before she sped off.

I didn't go to visit Grandma Harry much because, in a way, I agreed with Ashley—it was awfully depressing. Talking to her was sort of like talking to yourself, because she could no longer remember from one minute to the next. She might ask me how old I was now or how the weather was five times within a span of five minutes, but she could still remember the past vividly. Sometimes I liked to go talk to her about my father to hear her remember him as a little boy, as a man. There were times when she forgot that he was dead. So it was sort of like stepping into this little fantasy world where everything was still unbroken.

Still I paused at the door to her room for a minute, hesitant to step inside. I stared at the little placard on the door that said MRS. HARRIET MCALLISTER, thinking about how it looked awfully bold and official for a woman who was frail and shrunken and had a U-shaped spine.

There was a time, when I was younger and my grandpa Jack was still alive, that they'd had a house in Scottsdale, and my father used to drive us up there on the weekends. I don't remember much about it, but I remember Grandma Harry in the kitchen, wearing a red apron, putting trays of cookies in the oven. She wasn't a great cook, and she usually tried to make her cookies healthy by lacing them with bran and neglecting to tell us, so if you ate too many you'd spend a solid afternoon near the toilet. But for some reason I can remember the sound of her laughter, very clear and mellow and almost soothing, and I can remember that she had this blond hair that she sometimes had in rollers still, if we caught her too early in the morning.

This Grandma Harry, the one sitting up in the nursing-home bed, white hair thin enough to reveal red patches of skull bleeding out from underneath, skin wrinkled and shriveled and eyes slightly glazed, looked nothing like that other one, the one I knew so long ago that it felt like a dream.

"Melissa, honey, is that you?" I didn't know how long she watched me standing in the doorway before she said it, so I felt a little embarrassed as I stepped in.

"Hi, Grandma."

She reached her hands up for me, and I leaned over and gave her a kiss. "Oh, honey, I'm so happy to see you." She smelled like vinegar and pee, and I pulled away as quickly as I could and moved a chair up next to the bed. "Look at you. You're getting so big. How old are you now?"

"Fourteen."

"Oh my. Almost all grown up." She paused. "Where's your father?"

I stared at her, and for a second it felt like a game. Did she remember that he was dead or didn't she? Did I lie or tell the truth? "He's not here," I said, which was a compromise, not a lie but not really the truth either.

She sighed as if deep down she really knew, maybe in her heart, and I wondered if the heart held memories that the mind couldn't. "How's school?"

"It's good." I nodded. "I'm at the high school now."

"Oh good." She nodded, but I didn't think it meant anything to her one way or another what school I was at. "How's your sister?"

I rolled my eyes. "The same." Then I added. "She has a boyfriend."

"Oh my." She paused. "How old are you now, honey pie?"

"Fourteen."

"Oh my. Almost all grown up." I smiled, a big fake smile, baring my horse teeth, though I knew she wouldn't notice. Grandma Harry never cared what you looked like or if you had makeup on or if you'd done your hair or dressed up nice for her. *I love you for here and here,* she used to say as she put one hand on my head and the other on my heart.

"Did my father ever date anyone before my mother?" It was a question that had been burning up inside me all week, trying to imagine him with someone else, someone other than her, as if this would make her date okay, justifiable in a way.

"Oh, well, let me see." She closed her eyes. "Now that's going way back, isn't it?" She reached out for my hand, squeezed it. "Yes. There was a girl in college. What was her name? Oh, honey, my memory is terrible." I nodded. But I knew it was normally her short-term memory that was the problem; she couldn't remember the minute to minute, the day to day, but take her back twenty years, and she could usually tell you the tiny details of a moment. She opened her eyes. "Then, of course, there was Sally Bedford."

"Sally Bedford." I repeated it, rolled it around on my tongue a bit as if this would make it real, the idea of my father with someone who wasn't my mother.

"Where is your father?"

"I'm sorry," I told her, ducking the question. "I have to go." I leaned over and kissed her forehead.

"Thanks for coming by, honey pie," she said. "Come back soon."

"I will," I promised. I wondered, as I walked out, how many minutes it would take until she forgot I'd even been there.

chapter 5

After I inherited my father's journal, I decided I would keep a little journal of my own, where I would write down stories about people I knew, the way I imagined them to be. But it took me a while to figure out what to write, and the book stayed blank until the night when my mother had her first date. Then I decided I needed to start writing my parents' story, because I worried, if I didn't put it down on paper, that maybe no one would remember it, maybe it would disappear into something that had never even existed at all.

My Parents

The summer of 1986, when Cynthia Howard was Queen of the Rodeo, she worked as a candy striper in a hospital. This also happened to be the same summer that Tom McAllister, who was nearly finished with his degree in accounting, got appendicitis.

Tom's mother, Harriet, drove in from Scottsdale and nervously paced the floors of the waiting room as Tom went in for surgery. Tom was her baby, her only child, and she didn't care that he was nearly twenty-one and not suffering from all that serious of an ailment. She paced and she paced and she paced.

Cynthia watched her from down the hall, thinking that she must have something in her candy-striper cart to calm this woman down. A magazine, a teddy bear, a flower. "Hello," she said.

Harriet jumped. "Oh, hello, dear. I'm fine. Keep on keeping on." She waved Cynthia to go past her.

But Cynthia stopped. She put her hand on Harriet's shoulder. "I could get you a glass of water."

Then Harriet looked at Cynthia, really looked at her. She was stunning, with ivory skin that you just didn't see too much of in Arizona, and long, shiny black hair, a little pointy nose, and red lips, and she had such a warm smile that she *made Harriet feel all at once at ease. Harriet said, "Oh my, aren't you a beauty."*

Cynthia smiled. "How nice of you to say."

Harriet took a seat and patted the chair next to her. "Will you sit with me?"

It wasn't really Cynthia's job to sit in the waiting room like this. She was supposed to walk the halls and check on the patients, see if they needed any cheering up. But she supposed it couldn't hurt, for a few minutes. So she sat.

Harriet said, "I want to tell you about my son Tom." And she used words like handsome, magnificent, brilliant, funny.

Cynthia was not looking for a boyfriend. She wanted a pageant win and a scholarship to college. Her younger sister, Julie, would get a scholarship for being smart, but Cynthia knew she was going to have to get there by being beautiful.

But Cynthia let Harriet talk and talk and talk. Until the doctor came out to tell Harriet that Tom was fine, he was awake, and that she could see him.

By then Cynthia's shift was over, but she didn't have the heart to say so, so when Harriet asked her to come back with her and meet Tom, she agreed.

Tom was groggy from the anesthesia. And when he heard footsteps he looked up, and the first thing he saw was

Cynthia. "Am I dead?" he said to her.

"You'd better not be." Harriet marched into the room.

Cynthia hung back by the door and watched him. She could tell that Tom was serious, and his eyes were kind, and when he looked at her, it was as if she already was the Queen of the Rodeo, the most beautiful woman he'd ever seen.

Then there is the new story, the one that is not perfect, that is nothing like a fairy tale. As I hung out by the front window waiting for him to arrive, I tried to imagine the way it might have happened. Maybe as my mother razored up his sideburns their eyes caught for a minute—that would be all it would have taken. I tried to picture him ugly and bearded, fat and sarcastic. But I knew none of that would be true. My mother might be too old to be Queen of the Rodeo, but she was still stunning.

I got the phone and called Ryan while I was waiting. "My mother is getting ready for a date," I said when he picked up.

"Really? With who?"

"I don't know. Some guy she met at the salon."

"What's his name?"

I still had no idea, so I fashioned a nickname on the

spot. "I'm gonna call him the Hair."

Ryan laughed. "He could be bald."

"Then why was he at the salon in the first place?"

"Okay. It's the Hair then."

"You wanna ride bikes after she goes?"

He paused. "I can't. My dad's gonna be home soon, and he wants to go out to dinner."

"Well, okay then," I said. "Maybe tomorrow." It was hard to keep the flicker of annoyance out of my voice. I knew it wasn't his fault that his dad expected him to go out to dinner, but I wished he would've invited me to go along or promised to stop over afterward.

Ashley helped my mother pick out her outfit, a tiny little denim skirt that belonged to Ashley and a red shirt that really brought out her ivory skin. She had on strappy red sandals that made her legs look extra long. She did not look like someone's mother.

She was ready early, and then she paced by the front window as Ashley and I sat on the couch and watched her.

"This is silly, isn't it, girls? Maybe I should call and cancel."

"No," Ashley said. I glared at her, but I kept my

mouth shut because I really hoped my mother was serious and would decide to cancel on her own.

The three of us watched as he pulled into the driveway in a big, blue, shiny pickup truck. My dad had never really been a fan of pickup trucks. He used to say that he couldn't stand it when guys needed to show off how big and powerful and mighty they were by driving around in their huge vehicles and revving their engines.

When he started to get out, Ashley and my mother dragged me into the kitchen. "Don't let him see us watching," my mother whispered, as if he could already hear her.

I got my first glimpse of him when my mother opened the front door, and he stood there on our porch—tall, extraordinarily tan, clean shaven, completely handsome enough to be an underwear model, and, I was guessing, a good ten years younger than my mother. He had nice, thick black hair, and to my surprise, a good, neat-looking haircut. Maybe my mother knew what she was doing now.

He handed my mother a single long-stemmed purple rose. I looked to Ashley to see how she was reacting, and I was surprised to see that she looked a little stunned, as if the fact that he was beautiful changed everything. She hadn't expected a real prospect.

My mother took the rose. "Oh, how sweet. You shouldn't have. I love purple roses." She turned to look at us. "Girls, this is Kevin Baker."

I waved, and Ashley smiled at him and said, "Nice to meet you."

"Well, we won't be too late," my mother said.

My mother stepped out and shut the door behind them, and I was thinking about how she was walking into this whole new world, this entirely different life.

"I'm going out," Ashley said.

"Where?"

"None of your business." She paused. "Don't worry," she said. "It's not going to last, with Mom, I mean."

I nodded. "Well, I know that," I said, as if it were the most obvious conclusion in the world.

Then the house was quiet. Empty and eerily quiet. Not the good kind of quiet that comes after a storm but the bad kind that falls in the middle of loneliness.

I put a jar of Cheez Whiz in the microwave and sat at the kitchen table dipping potato chips into it for dinner. I was lucky that I had good metabolism, that I could eat whatever I wanted and I still stayed skinny, whereas

Ashley said she put on pounds just looking at half of what I ate. My mother always said my metabolism came from Grandma Harry, who used to eat a ton and was still as skinny as a rail. "Good genes, sweetie," she'd say.

I was obsessing over my mother's date, where they were, what they were doing, how much she was laughing, how much she was drinking. My mother couldn't hold her liquor. I'd seen her have a glass or two of wine with my father, and before you knew it she was crazy giddy, laughing and falling all over him. Do not have any wine, I silently willed her.

I was about halfway through the jar of cheese and starting to feel just a little bit sick when the doorbell rang. Ryan must've gotten back from dinner with his father and decided he wanted to hang out after all. I checked my hair in the hallway mirror, pulled it out of the hair band, and let it fall in little waves that hit my shoulders. I smiled, then frowned, and then whispered, "This is ridiculous." And I put my hair back in the ponytail. It would fly in my face if I rode my bike with it down.

The doorbell rang again, and I ran to get it, not even bothering to look through the peephole before I opened it, so I was shocked when it was not Ryan standing there but Courtney Whitman, holding on to a dog leash that was attached to a miniature Chihuahua. "Hey, Meliss."

"Hey." I tried to disguise my surprise.

"I was walking Paco and thought I'd stop by to say hi." As if on cue, at the sound of his name, Paco jumped up and barked a little.

"Hey there, boy." I reached down and rubbed his head, and I smiled to myself. Ryan was allergic to dogs.

"How did you know where I lived?" I asked.

"Oh." She laughed. "My mom's a realtor, so she knows where everyone lives." I didn't really think that was true, but I guessed they must have a way to look it up or something.

I noticed Courtney wasn't wearing any makeup like she normally did at school, and her hair was pulled back in a messy bun. She was wearing sweats and a tank top, and without all of that other stuff, the hoopla, as Grandma Harry used to call it, she wasn't even that pretty, just kind of normal-looking. "Well, what's up?" I asked.

She shrugged. "You wanna walk with me?"

It occurred to me that it was Saturday night, and here she was walking her dog and stopping at my house. Maybe it was harder for her to be new than I'd thought. "I guess so. Hang on. Let me get my key."

I shut the door, went back in the house, and scribbled

my mom a quick note, even though I was sure I'd be back first. Though she would expect Ashley to be gone, she might freak out if she came home and I wasn't in one of my usual spots on the couch or in my bed.

"How old's your dog?" I asked as we walked down the street, past Mrs. Keely's house, past Mr. and Mrs. Gonzalez, past Ryan's house.

"He's a puppy," she said. "My mom got him for me when we moved. It's supposed to help with the whole transition."

"Does it?"

She shrugged. "Sort of. Not really. I don't know." She paused. "Thanks for letting me share with you guys in biology the other day."

I felt a little guilty as I thought about how annoyed I'd been. "No problem," I said. "Anytime."

"So you and Ryan, you're like a couple, then?"

I felt a sinking in my stomach, as if the Cheez Whiz had just turned into this hard and crushing boulder. "No, no. Nothing like that. Just friends."

"Oh." She paused. "And you don't like him or any-thing?"

"Ryan? What? No way. Oh no. Definitely not." They were words I felt like choking on, because after I said them, I knew there was no taking them back. I was giving her permission to like him, to love him even, to claim him and take him for her own.

"I just don't want you to get mad at me if I go out with him or something. You're like the only friend I have here."

So we were friends. One shared dissection where I'd practically glared at her the whole time, and she considered us friends. There was something I loved about the ease of the whole thing, and something that seemed incredibly forced.

"You totally remind me of my best friend, Janie, back in San Diego." She sighed. "She was all serious and quiet and sweet like you."

I thought it was a compliment, but I wasn't sure. "Why did you move?"

She cringed. I could tell, even in the dark; her shoulders shrank. "My parents are getting divorced, and my mom wanted to be closer to my grandparents."

"That sucks," I said. I was tempted to tell her that my dad was dead and my mom was on a date, but I kept my mouth shut.

We'd walked a circle, and we ended up back in front of my house. "Hold out your hand," she said.

I did. She pulled a tiny little tube of lipstick out of her pocket, turned over my hand, and starting writing on the back of my palm. "Here's my number," she said. "Call me tomorrow."

Just before midnight I heard Ashley climbing in through her window, so I went and sat on her bed and waited for her.

The strange thing about Ashley was that even though she pretty much despised me most of the time, for whatever reason, she usually let me come in her room and hang out on her bed. Before she dated Austin and spent every single second with him, sometimes the two of us would lie on her bed and read magazines or do our homework. We hardly ever talked, and if we did, it was usually to insult each other.

She jumped and banged her hip on the dresser when she saw me. "Jesus, Melissa, you nearly gave me a heart attack."

She smelled like beer and cigarettes, two smells that were barely familiar to me but still distinct enough to detect. "You reek," I told her.

"Where's Mom?"

I shrugged.

"Wow." She sat down on the bed next to me. "She must really like him." She swallowed hard when she said it, so I could tell that deep down she was just as nervous about the whole thing as I was.

"You were the one that was all like, *I'll help you pick out your outfit. It'll be so great.*"

"Shut up." She swung her pillow at me, I ducked, and she missed me completely. "I was trying to be nice."

"Yeah, whatever."

We sat on the bed in silence for a few minutes, and I was about to get up and leave because I thought she'd already gone to sleep, when suddenly she said it, her voice suspended and calm, sounding more like my mother than her normal self. "Do you remember the time Dad took us on the boat?"

I didn't. Not really. I couldn't have been more than four or five at the time, and I remember there was lots and lots of blue water, everywhere you looked—the magnificent sparkle of Lake Mead, the opposite of every other desert landscape I'd ever seen. The water was so clear, and seemed to stretch for miles, that I thought the boat would take us to the end of the world.

"Did you know I almost drowned?"

I shook my head. "I knew you fell in. That's why you

never like to go swimming."

"I just remember being under the water, and it was so cold and rushing up all over. And then it was very dark, black even. Dad pulled me out. I opened my eyes, and he was carrying me, and he was crying. Did you know that? The man was freakin' crying. He loved me that much."

I closed my eyes, and I could picture it. My dad's round and serious face pulling Ashley from the water. But I had no memory of any of it. "Are you drunk?" I finally said.

"Get out." She threw the pillow at me again, and this time it smashed me in the head.

I heard my mom stumble in a few minutes later. I listened carefully, relieved to hear only one set of shoes, one set of footsteps. She'd come in alone. I heard her pouring water into the kettle for tea, and I thought about getting out of bed and going to sit with her in the kitchen, but I didn't really want to know, didn't want to see it on her face, if she was starting to fall in love with him.

chapter *6*

I'd written Courtney's number down on a Post-it on my desk after our walk, and the next morning, as I sat there trying to get my homework done, it was staring up at me. I wasn't sure why I would call it. I didn't want to be her friend; I didn't necessarily even like her. But then as I looked at the number, it didn't seem like it was an option not to call it.

It was after eleven and Ashley and my mother were both still in their beds. I'd already made a trip to the kitchen, spooned some peanut butter out of the jar, sat at the kitchen table, and sucked it down alone.

Before my father got sick, he used to cook us breakfast

on Sunday mornings. His specialty was French toast. He had this weird recipe where he'd put just a pinch of chili powder in with the cinnamon, something Grandma Harry had invented by accident when she once mixed up the two spices. It sounds terrible, but it was actually really, really good. My peanut butter on a spoon was no substitute.

When Courtney picked up, I said hi and I felt like an idiot. "It's Melissa."

"Hey, Meliss. What's up?"

"Not much." I tapped my pencil against the desk, realizing that I had absolutely nothing to say to her.

"I was just going to give myself a mani/pedi. Want to come over?"

"Okay. Sure," I said.

Courtney lived across the wash from us, in a development of new two-story homes. My development was built in the seventies, so our houses were brick with flat roofs that had this odd slant to them, so they sometimes looked like they could sink right into the ground. We had short driveways with painted metal carports, and black wrought-iron security doors in the front.

But just across the wash, there was Courtney's life, an

entirely different world. Big beige stucco houses with red tile roofs, long driveways, neat red rocks and trimmed shrubs out front. The houses in her neighborhood were much closer together than in mine, or maybe it just felt that way because they were so much bigger. Courtney lived just down the street from Austin and Ashley's best friend, Lexie, so in a way, as I biked across the wash, it was as if I was entering Ashley's world.

It was strange riding down the hill of the wash without Ryan. I hadn't been down there without him in a long time, probably years, and I knew if he knew I was going to Courtney's house he might be upset with me.

Courtney's house was like all the others on the street, very tall and clean and modern-looking, and she had a big stained-wood door in the front. I knocked on the door a few times. I heard Paco barking but no human sounds. Then I rang the bell. I had this moment, standing there on the porch, when I wondered if this was all some big joke that Ashley had set up, that Courtney wasn't actually home, that she didn't really think we were friends. And I was about ready to turn around and get on my bike when Courtney finally opened the door. Maybe she noticed the bewildered look on my face, because she said, "My mom is out, and I had my music up really loud." I nodded. "Come on in. I already picked out a polish color that'll look great with your skin."

I followed her into the house, down a long slate-tiled hallway, up a plushly carpeted staircase, into her bedroom. Her room was three times the size of mine and looked like something from one of those design magazines my mother read and sometimes left in the bathroom. She had this big canopy bed in the center with a pink silky-looking comforter and tons of expensive-looking pillows, and her bed was so high off the ground that she had a little step stool to get up.

She must have noticed me gawking because she sighed and said, "It's nice, isn't it? My mother's trying to buy me off so I don't miss San Diego."

"Do you? Miss it, I mean?"

She nodded. "Of course. This city is like, all dried up and in the middle of nowhere." She sighed. "No offense."

"Of course." I nodded, though I had little to compare it to, because I'd lived here all my life, aside from my three-month stint in Philadelphia, which was mostly spent in a hotel and a hospital waiting room. The warm desert air, the sparse landscapes, the brown mountains that turned purple against pink-blue skies at sunset all suddenly did seem a little dry and barren when I looked at the pictures of her in San Diego that she had all around the room—her at the beach with a bunch of other girls in tiny little bikinis, her standing in the driveway of what I assumed to be her old house, modest-looking with this patch of emerald grass out front.

"But I just hate being new at school. You know?"

I nodded.

"I had so many friends at my old school. I was voted most popular in the eighth-grade yearbook."

I nodded again like I knew all about what she was talking about. I had the urge to tell her that being friends with me or dating Ryan was not going to win her any popularity contests at our school, but I kept my mouth shut. There was something about her, this room, that drew me in, that made me actually want to paint my toenails and fingernails, something I usually had no interest in.

"Here, look at this color." She handed me a bottle of polish. Sugar Plum Fairy, a deep, rich purple. "What do you think?"

"It's nice," I said, though I had no opinion really.

"Take off your shoes," she said. I sat on the floor and obeyed, unlacing my old, grungy sneakers, trying to remember the last time I'd actually cut my toenails.

"Oooh, you have such nice feet," she said. "You should wear sandals more often."

"Do you think?" My feet looked sort of odd and calloused to me, but I wasn't a good judge of those kinds of things.

"Definitely." She held my foot in her lap and started painting carefully, with the hands of a skilled laborer who had done this a thousand times.

Two hours later I rode my bike back across the wash, with Sugar Plum Fairy nails as well as toenails, and I didn't feel like the same person. Maybe what my mother and Ashley said about how wearing makeup could boost your spirits was true, because I felt a lot better than I had when I'd left my house.

I was in my own little world, so I didn't even see Ryan out in front of his house at first. "Hey, Mel," he called, and his voice broke into my little fantasy world where people lived in perfect pink bedrooms. I hit the brakes and skidded to a stop in front of him. "You were riding in the wash without me?"

I hesitated for a minute wondering whether to lie or tell the truth, and before I could really decide, a lie popped out. "I was dropping off something for Ashley, at Mr. September's house."

"Why didn't she do it herself?"

"She wasn't feeling good."

He frowned, gave me a kind of suspicious sideways look. "What happened to your nails?"

"I painted them. Do you like them?"

"I guess." He shrugged, not nearly as convinced by the Sugar Plum Fairy as I'd been, which surprised me because I thought he'd be into that stuff, since he'd practically been drooling over Courtney in biology. I knew I would have to tell him about my friendship with her, but I wanted to keep it to myself for just a little bit longer.

"I have to go," I said, because I realized that my mom might be worried, that if she'd woken up and found my mysterious note that said "at a friend's house," she might be wondering what was taking me so long and who this friend was. And Ashley might be proclaiming that I must have been abducted by aliens, because I didn't have any real friends that she knew of.

"Wanna hang out later?" He called after me as I rode down the street.

"Sure," I yelled behind me. I no longer felt annoyed with him. In a weird way, I almost felt giddy.

◇

It was clear, as soon as I saw my mother sitting at the kitchen table with a cup of coffee and sunglasses on, that she had been drinking the night before, that she had in fact drunk too much, and that seemed like a very, very bad sign.

Ashley must've gotten up right before I got home, because she was at the table too, in her pajamas, her hair uncombed and sticking sideways, a half-eaten slice of honeydew on a plate in front of her.

"There you are," my mom said in what was probably meant to be her cheerful voice but came out all sort of muddled and groggy.

Ashley gasped. "You painted your nails!" She pretended to shiver. "Is it cold in here? Is hell freezing over?"

"Ashley, be nice." My mother pulled her sunglasses down the bridge of her nose and picked up my hands to examine them more closely. "Nice color, sweetie."

"Thanks," I said.

"Seriously." Ashley looked annoyed that no one was paying attention to her. "Since when do you paint your nails, Melissa?"

"My friend Courtney did them."

Ashley's eyes nearly bugged out of her head, and I knew immediately that she knew which Courtney I meant. Yes, I thought smugly, the new Courtney, beautiful and mysterious, and she was mine. "Courtney Whitman?" I could tell she couldn't believe it was true, even as she said it.

"Do you know her, sweetie?" my mom asked.

Ashley nodded. "Yeah, Max Healy is totally in love with her. Remember I was telling you?"

My mom had her sunglasses back on, so when she nodded, I couldn't tell if she really did remember or if she was only pretending. Sometimes I wondered how much my mom really listened to all the gossip Ashley told her or if, like me, she couldn't help but tune some of it out, let her mind wander to some other interesting and less-mundane place.

I knew who Max Healy was. Of course, everyone at my school knew who Max Healy was. He was one of Austin's best friends and a superstar on the football and baseball teams.

This knowledge that he liked Courtney made me feel incredibly joyful, because there was no way she would want Ryan once she found out about Max. Any girl would want Max. Even I'd felt a little tingly when

I walked by him in the hallway once and he gave me a smile. Max was just that kind of special guy.

"*You're* friends with Courtney." Ashley shook her head.

"Jealous?" I said.

"Whatever." She kicked my ankle hard under the table, so I retaliated by flicking her arm with one of my perfect Sugar Plum nails. "Oww. Melissa."

"Girls." My mother held on to her head. "Please."

Ashley turned and stuck her tongue out at me as she pranced off to her room. "Real mature," I called after her. But I could not wipe this crazy, silly grin off my face for the rest of the day.

chapter 7

The Monday morning after I went to her house for the first time, Courtney sat out on the front steps of Desert Crest High waiting for me and Ryan to bike up. "Hey, guys." She gave a little wave when she saw us coming.

"Is she waving to us?" Ryan said, the disbelief as thick and heavy as his asthmatic breath after coming up the hill.

"Yep. I do believe she is," I said, sort of smugly.

She linked arms with me as we walked up those front steps, which gave me an entirely different feeling about the place. People were watching me. I felt their eyes. And not strange stares but interested ones, and this made me hold my head up a little higher as I went to my locker.

Ryan trailed behind us, looking just a little lost at first, until Courtney stopped, touched his shoulder, and whispered something in his ear that made him laugh. That laugh cut me, just a little bit; it started a tiny pang of something shooting through my chest. But I was determined to ignore it. I couldn't blame Ryan for being taken with her, when clearly, I was too.

In biology Courtney forced Jeffrey to join our lab table, so it really ended up being the three of us working on Kermit, while Jeffrey was left to have a go of it with his and Courtney's frog on his own. "Hey, Courtney, don't you want a turn to cut?" he kept saying and waving the scalpel in the air, sort of Jeffrey Dahmer–like.

"Ewww. I don't think so." She made a face at me, as if to say, *Is he not the most disgusting boy you've ever met?* And I rolled my eyes to commiserate, but deep down I felt just a little sorry for him.

I started hanging out at Courtney's house after school, finding an odd sort of peace in her beautiful bedroom. I changed my nail color six times in three weeks, a fact that Ashley just could not get over, and my mother seemed a little proud of. She got this funny smile when she looked at me, as if she were thinking, Hmmm, maybe this girl did get some of my DNA after all.

In this same time, I did not look in my dad's journal at all. I had no new tidbits rolling around in my brain, nothing interesting to contemplate.

Instead there were other things: Courtney and I spent an entire afternoon trying to find the perfect shade of lipstick from her collection to match my skin tone. She finally decided on one with a reddish tint that tasted fruity, called Apple of My Eye, that she said really complemented my paler skin. "Here. Take it home with you," she said.

"No, seriously. I can't."

"Go ahead." She shoved the tube in my hand and closed my fingers around it. "It looks way better on you than it does on me anyway."

Still, in my bedroom, in front of my own mirror, I thought it looked silly on me, as if I were a little kid trying to play dress-up, and I put it in my jewelry box and told myself I'd take it out for special occasions only.

Some days after school we'd spend an hour or so in Walgreens looking through the makeup and scented lotions and perfumes, and Courtney always swore she needed my opinion, even though, really, I had no idea what I was talking about and usually just ended up agreeing with whatever she said.

"Which do you like better?" she'd ask, pouring a little tester of two lotions on her arms, one on each wrist. "The peach," she'd answer herself. "Yes, definitely a little sexier."

I wasn't exactly sure what made peach so sexy, but I nodded and murmured in agreement. Courtney always had her mother's credit card, so she could buy whatever she wanted and a lot of it, whereas I had some spare lunch-money change in my pocket that wouldn't get me much more than a pack of gum.

The interesting thing about Courtney was that in addition to being incredibly beautiful, she was also really goofy. She liked to hang upside down from the bar in her gigantic closet, she knew how to knit and made all these cute little outfits for Paco, and though she was kind of an idiot in biology, she had this amazing memory for words and could quote from almost anything she'd ever read.

"Clothes make the man," she'd said as she knitted, and then she put down her needles and pushed Paco's ears toward his face so he had a funny little look. "Probably not what Twain meant." She'd laughed.

She had me laughing one day as I was sitting on her

floor painting my toenails Heavenly Plum, and she was painting Paco's toenails Perfect Peach, so I just blurted out what Ashley had told me, without really even thinking about it. "You know Max Healy is in love with you."

She stopped painting Paco's toenails for a moment, crinkled up her nose, and laughed. "Guys like Max are a dime a dozen."

I froze, the nailbrush suspended in midair until I realized it was about to drip on her carpet and I quickly shoved it back into the bottle. "Why would you say that?"

"I dated a guy, Mark, just like him at my old school. And every time I went out with him, I swear all he wanted to do was grab my boobs."

Courtney, unlike me, had very nice, perfect-looking boobs, and she wore a lot of V-neck shirts and bras that pushed them up and gave her a little bit of cleavage. "But Max is . . . Max."

"I know. I know." She paused. "But Ryan is so cute." She sighed. "Do you think I even have a chance with him?"

I nodded and smiled, and I knew I was baring my horse teeth because it hurt to keep smiling. "Of course you do."

"Will you get him to ask me out? Oh please, please, please, Meliss."

I wasn't quite sure how we'd gotten here, from me innocently telling her what Ashley had said about Max. But here we were, the moment I knew had been coming since the time Courtney and I had taken Paco around the block a few weeks earlier, even though I hadn't quite let myself believe it. "Of course," I said, still smiling. "Of course I'll do that."

She put Paco on the ground and leaned over and crushed me in a hug. "You're the best, Meliss. You really are."

It was dark by the time I rode across the wash; the Heavenly Plum on my nails seemed invisible, the way I felt riding my bike in the pitch black of the desert. I wondered how long I could put Courtney off, and whether it really mattered if I did or not. It seemed inevitable that she and Ryan were going to become a couple, and then they were going to spend all their time together and there would be no more manicures on Courtney's floor, no more bike rides with Ryan.

Ashley was sitting at the kitchen table with a half-eaten bowl of ramen noodles when I walked in. "Let me see." She grabbed my hands and examined the plum color in the pale fluorescent light of the kitchen. "Not bad."

"Where's Mom?"

"Out with Kevin."

"Again?" If I was counting accurately, this was date number five, but I knew there could be others, times I didn't even know about. I grabbed a spoon, sat down next to Ashley, and dug into her half-eaten soup. "It can't last forever, right?"

"I don't know." Her voice was quiet, so I could tell she honestly didn't. And really, how much did it mean to her anyway? One more year and she'd be away at college, and then I'd be stuck here all by myself with my mom and some guy she was dating or, God forbid, even marrying. And it hit me, that when Ashley was gone, I might actually miss her.

"Courtney likes Ryan," I blurted out, a confession.

"Oh." It surprised me that she didn't laugh or make fun of me, but still I didn't want to look up, so I concentrated really hard on the soup.

The front door opened and my mom walked in. "Hi, girls." She looked a little sad, maybe like she'd been crying, and her hair was messy and falling out of her ponytail. I looked at Ashley, who shrugged her shoulders. "I'm exhausted. I'm going straight to bed. Okay, girls?"

We nodded. "Good night," Ashley said.

"Yeah," I chimed in. "'Night."

Ashley and I sat there quietly for a few minutes. I'd finished her soup and I was still hungry, but I didn't feel like moving to find something else. "You know what you need?" she finally said.

"What?"

"A boyfriend. Something to make Ryan jealous."

"I don't want to make him jealous."

She laughed. "Of course you do." It amazed me how easy it was for her. "You know, if you let Mom fix your hair up and you wore a little more makeup and a push-up bra and . . . well, you wouldn't be half bad."

"Gee, thanks." But what surprised me was that there was something in there that sounded like a promise.

After Ashley went to bed, I sat up for a while at my desk doing my homework. I thought about what Ashley had said, that I needed a boyfriend, and it was the first time I'd ever really thought about it. I mean, really thought about it. It's not that I'd never been interested in a boy before.

There was this one guy I'd liked, Justin Mannor. Just before we'd left for Philadelphia, Kelly Jamison had her first-ever boy-girl birthday party, and he'd been there. Kelly had told him that I liked him, and as we all played around in the pool, he came up behind me and covered my eyes with his hands, and whispered *Boo*. I jumped, but I felt all warm and tingly with him standing so close to me. But that was it: By the time we came back, he had another girlfriend, some girl named Tess who played field hockey and was all lean and muscular.

I'd never really seriously thought about dating, though, not exclusively anyway, the way Ashley was with Austin.

I pulled out a blank piece of paper and decided I'd make a list of boys at my school who I would want to date. I wrote Max Healy's name at the top, because despite what Courtney said, any girl at my school would want to date him. But after that, I was stuck.

I heard a tap-tapping on the window, and I jumped and then panicked and tore up the piece of paper.

I went over to open the window and Ryan climbed in. "What's up?" he said.

Though he'd climbed into my room this way probably a thousand times, this time I felt my heart beating, my palms beginning to sweat. "Not much." I tried to sound nonchalant. "Math."

He made a face and plopped down on my bed. He stretched out so far that his feet hung off the edge. He was so tall now that I bet he would've even been taller than my dad, who'd been no slouch at six feet.

"Do you wanna ride?" I asked him.

He shrugged. "If you want to."

I didn't really, but I didn't feel like sitting here in my room with him either. If we started talking, I knew I would have to tell him about Courtney, that I would blurt it out the way I had with Ashley earlier, and I wanted to keep it to myself for as long as possible.

So I jumped out the window, and he followed behind me. I heard his footsteps, his thick breath as we ran to our bikes, hopped on, and started riding.

It was getting cooler at night now, and as we got down in the wash, I started to shiver. The cold, dry air bristled over me and brought goose bumps to my arms. I should've gotten a sweatshirt, but I wasn't going to go back for it.

We rode together down the wash, our legs pumping harder, faster, until I was cold and sweating all at once, and I got that strange prickly sensation that I'd sometimes get right before I was about to vomit. When we got close to the railroad tracks we both stopped and hung on to our handlebars to catch our breath.

Once we were still for a few minutes, I started shivering again. "You're cold?" Ryan said.

"No," I lied. "I'm fine."

He sat up and pulled his sweatshirt over his head. "Here." He handed it to me.

I shook my head. "No. I'm fine. Really. That's okay."

"You're shaking, Mel. Take it."

I didn't think he was going to take no for answer, so I did.

Ashley and Austin

When Ashley was fifteen her father died of cancer, and six weeks later, just after school let out for the summer, Ashley curled her hair, put on her red lipstick, pasted on a smile, and entered her first beauty pageant. She did not win. She did not even come in second. In fact, she came in second to last, and as she looked around she realized she was the fattest girl there. "Don't worry, sweetie," her mother told her with sad and anxious eyes. "There's always next time."

Ashley spent the summer eating raw carrots and lemon-water ice, and by the time school started again, her mother had to take her shopping for a whole new size-0 wardrobe. Her hip bones were pointy, like little darts, and her stomach was so flat that even when she sat down she didn't bulge a bit. Over the summer, she'd grown her hair long and learned how to really use an eye pencil to make her green eyes look large and piercing.

In the fall she entered another beauty pageant, and this time she came in second place, which got her a fifty-dollar gift certificate to Target, a red sash that she would hang on the wall in her room, and instant popularity at school.

She became friends with a bouncy-headed cheerleader (Bobblehead) and a rich girl whose father bought her a nose job for her sixteenth birthday (the Nose). Ashley asked her mother for a nose job when she turned sixteen in the spring, but what she got instead were the keys to her father's old Camry.

The Nose had a crush on one of the baseball players, so she dragged Ashley to the practices after school. The first time Ashley saw Austin, he was pitching, his long and lean body curled up and then stretched out so he looked like a cat. He didn't notice Ashley that day, or the next one, or the next.

But his friend George Henkins noticed the Nose. And he asked her out, and for some odd reason, despite the fact that he'd given her a nose job, her father didn't want her to date alone. So the Nose invited Ashley on their date, and George invited Austin.

At the end of the night, Austin walked Ashley to the front door and asked if he could call her. He kissed her once, sweetly on the cheek—or at least, this is the version of the story Ashley told her mother.

In another version—which Ashley told the Nose on the phone after she thought her mother and sister had gone to bed—Ashley let Austin kiss her in the dark front seat of her car and didn't stop him when he slid his hand up her shirt.

After our fleeting moment at the kitchen table the night before, when I woke up the next morning, I almost expected things to be different with Ashley and me. But she didn't offer to drive me to school. She didn't say anything to me at all except when she frowned and said, "That's what you're wearing?"

"What?" I didn't see anything wrong with my broken-in, comfortable jeans, my white shirt, and hooded sweatshirt.

She sighed, grabbed a banana and the car keys, and she left.

My mother sat at the table nursing her coffee, but she said nothing. I was hopeful, after the way she'd seemed the night before, that Kevin had broken up with her. But she didn't say anything of the sort. In fact, she didn't say much at all. She looked a little old sitting there, and tired, and all worn out, as if life had stretched her just a little too much in the past few years and she wasn't exactly sure how to spring back anymore. "Are you okay?" I finally asked her.

She smiled. "Just a little tired, sweetie." She paused, started to say something, then stopped.

"What?"

"Oh, it's nothing. I just stopped by to see Grandma Harry yesterday for her birthday."

Her birthday. I'd completely forgotten and probably earned Worst Granddaughter of the Year award, although I was tied with Ashley because I was sure she hadn't remembered either.

"It's just so depressing to see her that way. Honest to God. I—"

"She didn't remember. Did she?"

She shook her head. "And I didn't have the heart to say it to her, to make her feel it all over again." She reached across the table and squeezed my hand.

Even thinking about it, fresh tears sprang to my eyes. I pictured him lying in the hospice bed, then another time, a time when he was whole, when he was laughing and telling me in his crazy, excited voice about some new fact he'd uncovered. I could hear his voice, the way he called me Melon, so I was this interesting, fun person that I never was with anybody else.

There were a lot of questions hanging in the air—did my mother still remember him as vividly as I did, did she still miss him, was she really serious with this Kevin guy?—but I didn't say a word. Finally, she said, "You'd better get going. You don't want to be late for school."

chapter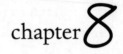

By the end of October, Kermit was a mess, barely recognizable as a frog at all, just a pile of cuts and dried-up innards, and hardly even suitable to study, which is what we were supposed to be doing in preparation for the end-of-the-marking-period exam.

I was trying to study, diligently looking back and forth between the carcass and my diagram, but it was hard to concentrate with Courtney hanging all over Ryan, whispering things in his ear and making him laugh.

Finally, Jeffrey said, "Why don't you two just get a room already?" He rolled his eyes at me, but I hastily looked away, not wanting to be seen commiserating with him on any sort of level.

His comment sent Courtney into a fit of uncontrollable giggles and made Ryan turn bright red. I pretended to be really, really studying the frog because I didn't want to have to look at either one of them, to see Ryan's nervous stare or Courtney's anxious one. No. No. No. Frog parts. Think frog parts.

"Ladies and gentlemen, do you find dead frogs funny?" Courtney had giggled for so long and so loud that Mr. Finkelstein had actually gotten up out of his desk chair and made his way to our table.

"No, sir," Ryan said, and he pulled his goggles back down. He pretended to concentrate really hard on the frog. I could hear his breathing speed up, something that might be undetectable to anyone else but that I knew meant he might be heading toward an asthma attack.

"You all right?" I whispered to him.

He nodded, not taking his eyes off the frog for one second.

I was a little late meeting Ryan after school. I didn't always rush right out of English when the bell rang last period. Sometimes Mrs. Connor was finishing a thought, and she was interesting enough that the majority of us let her without jumping out of our seats and rushing for the door.

Today we'd been talking about tragic heroes. "Every tragic hero has hamartia," Mrs. Connor said. "Their tragic flaw." She paused dramatically. "And this is what causes them to fall from greatness." She was wearing a red feather boa, and she swung it quickly around her neck as if to emphasize her point.

I wondered if it was really true, that every hero had to have this. It seemed impossible that there could not be at least one hero who remained entirely and truly heroic and did not succumb to some great flaw. But as Mrs. Connor said, heroes were just human beings, like the rest of us.

By the time I got out front to the bike racks, the school had emptied out considerably, and the throngs of people that usually cluttered up the front steps were already well out into the parking lot and the street. So it was easy to spot Ryan, to see it all clearly.

He was hanging over the handlebars of his bike with his back toward me, and Courtney was facing in my direction, leaning toward him. She had on this really tight pink shirt that showed every ounce of perfect cleavage as she leaned over.

I watched the two of them from my spot on the steps, and I knew just what was about to happen. Then it started to unfold, as if in slow motion. Courtney leaned in closer, closer, until I could no longer see her face clearly because it was on top of his, her lips on his, and they were kissing. Not a short, cute little peck, but a long, drawn-out Ashley-and-Austin-against-the-lockers kiss. My first odd thought was that Courtney was Ryan's hamartia.

I knew I was going to have to get my bike, but I didn't want to walk over in the middle of the kiss, so I just stood on the steps for a few minutes. I tried not to stare, but every time I peeked back, they were still kissing.

Ashley and the Nose tumbled down the steps behind me. I didn't see them at first until Ashley elbowed me in the ribs. "Stare much?" she said. The Nose started laughing.

I glared at her.

Maybe Courtney heard the Nose laughing, because she pulled back, looked around for a minute, and then waved at me. "Oh hey, Meliss." I waved back.

"You should totally kick her ass," the Nose whispered to me, and Ashley started giggling, as if trying to imagine me kicking anyone's ass was an entirely ridiculous thought.

Ryan still hadn't looked up, and I knew he wasn't going to.

I walked over and grabbed my bike. "I gotta get home," I said, trying to sound nonchalant, as if I didn't have a care in the world. "See ya."

I hopped on my bike and rode down the hill so fast that I felt like I was flying. It was an out-of-control, scary kind of fast, so I knew I couldn't stop it even if I wanted to, this wild, nauseating ride.

And I rode and I rode.

Past my house. Past Ryan's. I kept riding. Not sure how to stop, not sure if I wanted to, until I found myself in the parking lot of Sunset Vistas, and I knew I was going to go in and visit with Grandma Harry.

I was sweating when I chained my bike outside. The warm October sun had been beating down on me all the way over here, but the funny thing was, I hadn't really even noticed until I stopped.

Grandma Harry was eating lime Jell-O and watching *General Hospital* when I walked in. The TV was blasting, up at least ten notches too loud, the way I noticed it always was with old people. "Oh, Melissa, honey. I haven't seen you in ages."

"I'm sorry." I leaned down and kissed her, but I already felt sort of defeated, knowing she didn't even remember my most recent visit.

"How old are you now?"

"Fourteen."

"Oh my, you're so old now." She put down the Jell-O and held her hands up to her face. "Where has the time gone?"

"What's going on on *GH*?"

"Oh this." She waved her hand. "I'm only half paying attention. Sometimes I just sit here and daydream, you know, and these dang shows just come on. Background noise."

"Happy Birthday."

"Is it really my birthday?"

"Yesterday it was. Sorry I'm late." Even when Grandma Harry had remembered everything, she lied about her birthday. No one ever really knew how old she was, except for my mother, who'd come across her birth certificate when she helped her move from Scottsdale down here into assisted living. And she had sworn on the grave of my grandpa Jack that she would never reveal my grandmother's real age, so to Ashley and I, it still remained a mystery. At last count, she may have said somewhere around seventy-five, but my guess was that she was really closer to eighty.

"Oh, honey pie. It's so good to see you." She grabbed my hand, squeezed it, and held on tight. "Thank you for coming. So tell me, what's new with you?"

I knew I could talk to her honestly, and she probably wouldn't remember much of what I was saying to repeat it to my mother or Ashley, but I still couldn't find the words to get out the truth. So I said, "Well, not too much."

"How's school?"

"We're dissecting a frog in biology."

She made a face. "That sounds positively inhumane, honey pie."

"It's not so bad," I lied.

"How's your beautiful family?"

I thought about Ashley elbowing me on the steps of the school, and my mother off on a date with Kevin, but I just told her that we were all doing great.

She stared at me for a moment, then frowned. "You have sad eyes, honey pie." It was strange how so much of her mind was missing, but she still seemed to notice me more than anyone else had lately.

"Do I?"

She smiled at me and nodded as if saying, *It's okay, you can tell me everything*, and a part of me wanted to. She was my father's mother, after all, my only real blood connection to him other than Ashley, and Ashley didn't seem to count. "Sometimes I feel like everyone's leaving me," I whispered.

She grabbed my hand and squeezed it. "Oh, honey pie. I'm right here, aren't I?"

I nodded, though I was thinking that she wasn't. Not really. Not the person that she was or might've been. Just this old lady who kind of looked like my grandmother but couldn't always remember exactly what it meant to be here.

We sat there quietly, just staring at each other, until she smiled and said, "Now tell me, how's your beautiful family?"

"We're fine," I whispered. "Fine. Fine." I forced a smile, and I stood up.

It felt pointless to repeat myself, to talk into nothing, to feel that everything I said sat in her brain for a moment until it vanished into dust. I leaned down and hugged her. "Happy birthday," I said. "I'll come back soon."

"Oh please do," she said. "I can't tell you how much this means to me."

◇

I took the long way home because I wanted to ride, wanted to pedal and pedal and pedal and push harder and faster. I was really sweating by the time I got in the house, so I took a soda out of the fridge and took it into my room to drink it.

I turned on the ceiling fan, and I took off my shirt, which was soaked through with sweat, and I rummaged in my drawers until I found an old bikini top of Ashley's. And then I sat on the floor and flipped through my dad's journal. I hadn't picked it up in a few weeks, but now I needed it again. Needed it to give me hope or inspiration or an iota of what I'd actually gotten from him when he was still alive.

I read through a few pages, trying to find something interesting, something that would make me laugh or see things differently. That's what I loved about his facts and his stories, the way they made you think about things that you never ever thought to think before, as if to remind you that there was always some completely new way to look at the world.

I found this one story about an eighty-nine-year-old woman named Ida Mae who went skydiving for the first time when she married a sixty-year-old skydiving instructor. It's the kind of eighty-nine-year-old I would've imagined Grandma Harry to be if she wasn't stuck inside Sunset Vistas, her memory cells falling away by the second.

Then I turned the page, to a list of random facts about weather. I learned that lightning strikes six thousand times a minute and that men are six times more likely to be struck than women. I thought about the summer monsoon storms, the great big bolts of lightning that lit up our sky, our city. We could watch them, high above the mountaintops, beautiful and dangerous all at the same time, from our back patio.

Just before my father got sick, one of those lightning strikes hit a tree in a forest on top of one of the mountains that surrounds us. It ended up burning thousands of acres and most of a small town before it sizzled out. We saw the cloud of smoke, big and thick and oddly white and puffy, hanging up above the mountain for weeks.

It was there when we went to Dr. Singh's office that day and found out that something terrible had happened in my father's body too. That's the way my father first explained his illness to me. "It's kind of like the fire, Melon. Right now it's burning out of control. But the doctors are going to try to stop it. They're going to give me medicine to keep it from spreading."

The next week my father started his treatment, and I came to learn that by "medicine" he meant chemo, and with chemo there was another kind of destruction: hair that fell away in clumps, pale skin that stretched across a body that became bony and way too thin when it couldn't hold down food.

Dr. Singh was a short, skinny, dark-haired man who looked nothing like a firefighter, which confused me for a few weeks. But then a miraculous thing happened. The firefighters finally won, the smoke died down, the forest stopped burning.

When the road up the mountain reopened and my father was between rounds of chemo, he drove me up there. The devastation startled me—all the beautiful evergreen and oak trees stripped bare, the world of the forest, ashy and dead-looking.

"One little strike of lightning, Melon," my dad mused, "and look at all of this."

I wondered if that's when my dad found the facts about lightning, that week, just on the brink of something terrible. I pictured the way the facts might make him feel better, might make him calmer. Lightning was so common, and very rarely did it destroy as badly as it had on the mountain.

I closed the journal and put it back on my desk, and then I noticed a little piece of paper on my floor that must have fallen out of the front pocket of the book. I picked it up and opened it and read it over a few times trying to figure out exactly what it might mean. It said, *Call Sally Bedford*. Sally Bedford. The woman Grandma Harry had mentioned to me, that I'd assumed was one of my father's college girlfriends. But then what was he doing with a note to call her in his journal?

I heard the doorbell ringing somewhere in the distance, so I put the piece of paper back inside the journal before I went to answer it. I wasn't thinking about the fact that I was still in a bikini top and jeans, because there was something about that note, written in my dad's familiar scrawling strokes that really unnerved me. And I wasn't even thinking to check who was at the door, because I just assumed it was going to be Ryan or Courtney or the both of them.

So I opened it annoyed and only half paying attention, and when I looked up I saw Max Healy standing on my front porch. Suddenly, I remembered the bikini top. I tried to fold my arms over my chest sort of nonchalantly as if I always stood that way.

Max whistled, and I felt myself turning red. "Who are you?" he said, which was a strange question, considering he was the one who rang my doorbell.

Ashley and the Nose must have been in her bedroom, because I heard them barreling down the front hallway until they were close enough to the door to push me out of the way. "Hey, Max," Ashley said in that supersweet voice she usually reserved for Austin, so I wondered if they'd broken up. Maybe he would become Mr. October after all. "Come on in." Ashley glared at me, and I knew she wanted me to leave, but I didn't.

"Who's that?" Max pointed to me.

The Nose laughed. "That's Ashley's sister. And she was just leaving, weren't you?" Ashley glared at me again and motioned with her head toward the front door, but I didn't know where she expected me to go dressed like this.

"Hey." Max gave me a little wave.

I felt my heart pounding as I waved back to him. "See ya," I said, and I turned on my heels and headed back toward my room.

"Don't pay any attention to her," I heard Ashley say.

Yes, don't pay any attention to me. I'm invisible.

chapter *9*

I came to learn that there is an awful lot you don't want to know that you can learn on the internet. If I wasn't feeling well or I developed a symptom, I tended to go a little overboard and look it up on Google. Then I'd end up on some website for some strange disease, which I would convince myself that I had in a matter of minutes.

Right after my dad died, I got this weird eyelid twitch, which was really annoying. My bottom lid would just twitch and twitch, no matter what I did to try and stop it. I looked it up online and settled on Parkinson's disease. I told my mother that I needed to go for an MRI.

"I'm sure you're fine, sweetie." She brushed me off, the way she did about most things.

"Look at it." I pointed to my eyelid, which had started twitching like crazy while I talked to her.

"That happens to me when I get tired," she said, all nonchalantly, not even caring that I may or may not have this terrible disease.

I sighed. "But I have a bad feeling about it."

She stopped what she was doing, came over, and gave me a hug. She pulled back and looked directly at me. "I'll tell you what, sweetie. Let's give it a few weeks and see if it goes away on its own first." I could hear it in her voice, that my mother was sick of doctors, that she couldn't believe that there could really be anything wrong with me, that lightning would strike us twice. I didn't want to be the one to take her back to that awful place again, so I nodded.

She was right; the twitch did stop after a few weeks, and after that I promised myself that I wouldn't look up any more symptoms on the internet.

But it was hard to stop. Especially if something was bothering me, if I was home all alone with nothing else to think about. I didn't mention anything else to my mother though. I figured each time that I would do what she said and see if it got better on its own in a few weeks. And each time I held my breath, waiting for something to subside: stomach pain (appendicitis or an ulcer), sore throat and swollen glands (lymphoma), pain in my chest (a clogged artery).

The pains all went away, some slowly, some quickly, but the fear did not, the knowledge that a terrible disease could creep up on you at any second, that it could blindside you and take everything, swiftly and all at once.

So you would think after all the worrisome information I'd found on the internet, I might have thought twice before Googling Sally Bedford. But I didn't. Her name burned my brain, and it made my head hurt. I sat there, my throbbing head in one hand, the scrap of paper with her name in the other, and I debated whether I should try to figure out if I could have a brain tumor or if I should try to figure out who she was. I picked the second choice.

It seemed like it would be a common name, but the first entry that popped up was for a Sally Bedford who worked at Charles and Large Accountants. No, that couldn't be right. She couldn't have worked at the same accounting firm as my dad. I would've heard of her before.

I clicked on the website, and it took me to the C & L site, with a page that had pictures of their employees. Sally Bedford, it read under her name, senior office manager. The picture of her was grainy and small, so it was hard to see what she really looked like, but she wasn't beautiful, not even close to my mother.

Her hair was a mousy brown. She had olive skin and green eyes and this pointy little chin and a button nose that looked a little small for her face. It was as if someone had taken all of her features and squashed them incorrectly, because she looked entirely out of proportion. I wondered what her story was—and if it was interesting enough for my father to include in his notes, or if it was something he'd decided to pass up on. It was the only reasonable explanation I could think of for why he would have a note to call her in his journal.

What Grandma Harry said still gnawed at me. But she must have gotten confused. Or maybe Sally Bedford was the name of a girl he'd dated in college and she'd ended up working at the same accounting firm, which didn't really explain why he had that note in his book.

I felt this anger at him, my father. It boiled up in my chest and burned my throat, giving me this terrible acidic taste in my mouth. It wasn't fair that he wasn't here for me to ask him, for him to make the worry subside. I imagined the way it might have gone:

"Hey, Dad. Can I ask you something?"

"What is it, Melon? You know you can ask me anything."

"Well, who's Sally Bedford? Grandma said you dated her and I found her name in your book."

He'd laugh—I could still remember the sound of his laughter, big and roaring in a way that reminded me of a lion. "Dated her? Why, if you consider doing someone's taxes dating them, I'd have racked up quite a few women over the years."

But that didn't make any sense; why would Grandma Harry know about her then?

"Dated her? Her parents own Sunset Vistas, and she helped us get Grandma Harry in. You know how easily she gets attached to people." He'd laugh again and shake his head, as if to say that Grandma Harry was a nut job, but still he loved her all the same.

But he wasn't here. So there was no one to ask, no easy explanations.

I crumpled up the piece of paper and threw it in my trash can. What difference did it make now anyway? I crawled into my bed, climbed under the covers, and put the pillow over my throbbing head.

I fell into a deep sleep, and I had a dream about him. He was riding on my bike down the wash, and I was trying to keep up with him on foot, but he was just out of my reach, just ahead of me. I stopped running and put my head down to catch my breath. "Don't give up," he said to me as he kept on pedaling, fast enough to make it to the end of the Earth.

I woke up tangled in sheets and sweating.

The next morning, the first thing I did when I got out of bed was take the paper out of my trash can, smooth it out, and put it back inside the journal. If there was one thing my father loved, it was a good mystery.

My mother hated mysteries. She didn't have the patience to sift through the clues, to make it to the end, the answer, but like my father I loved to watch things unravel in such a way that they made sense.

I was almost surprised to find Ryan waiting for me in the street on his bike when I walked outside, and then I felt a little silly thinking that one kiss with Courtney was going to make him ditch me. "Hey," he said when he saw me, but he didn't exactly meet my eyes.

"Hey." I hopped on my bike and we started riding next to each other up the street toward the hill. We didn't say anything else for a few minutes, until finally I said, "So you and Courtney are like a couple now or something?"

He shrugged. "Not really. I don't know." I knew he was thinking that Courtney wouldn't ever want to date him, really date him in an Ashley/Austin sort of way. The knowledge that she did was burning up in my brain, this secret so heavy that it wanted to explode right out of me, but I kept it inside anyway.

Instead, I changed the subject. "I think my father had a secret."

"Yeah? What makes you think that?"

"I don't know. Just something I found in his journal. And something my grandmother said."

"Isn't she, you know, a little loony tunes?" He lifted up a hand and twirled his finger in the air.

"No." I felt insulted for her. It must be awful to be so old and instantly dismissed just because you couldn't remember. "She's just a little forgetful."

He rolled his eyes.

"What?"

"I don't know," he said.

"Say it."

It took him a minute. We rode up the hill, and he started breathing extra hard, so by the time he did finally say it, his words were heavy. "Mel, he's been dead a year and a half."

"So?"

"Well, I don't know. Just forget it."

I knew what he was implying, that once you were dead your secrets no longer mattered, that there was only so long you could hold on to the past before it consumed you, until it ate you up and swallowed you whole. But it mattered to me. My father's secrets were still important, worth knowing, because in a way that was all I had left of him, some sort of odd legacy.

But before I could say anything else, we pulled up in front of the school. Courtney was already standing on the front steps. She waved to me and then ran up to Ryan and gave him a big hug. "Hey, Ry," she gushed. She turned to me. "Hey, Meliss." It was annoying, that habit she had of shortening our names in peculiar ways.

Courtney was hanging on him, and she whispered something in his ear that made him laugh. I chained my bike to the rack. "I'll see you guys inside," I said, but neither one of them seemed to hear me. I slipped quietly past them and walked down the hall to my locker alone.

I had my head in there, putting in books I didn't need and pulling out ones I did, when I heard a tapping on the metal door. I looked up.

Staring right at me, his big brown eyes all sparkly and sweet-looking, was Max Healy. "Hey there, Ashley's sister." He smiled. He had this sort of cocky smile that seemed to say he knew just how gorgeous and nice and funny he was, and if you couldn't recognize it, well then, too bad. He also had really, really nice teeth. Short and square and not at all horselike.

"I have a name," I said, surprised by the no-nonsense sound of my voice, because I hadn't thought the words through before they popped out of my mouth.

"A secret name?"

I felt my neck getting hot, and I knew it would only be a matter of seconds before the flush spread across my face and I was completely bright red. "Melissa," I finally mumbled, and then looked back into the locker as if I were searching for something very urgent, which, unless you were counting piles of old gum wrappers and balled-up math homework, I wasn't.

When I looked up again, he was gone.

I spent most of the afternoon picking off my red nail polish. I did it meticulously, so that by English last period there were only a few tiny specks of red remaining on my left pinkie. As soon as the bell rang, I jumped up and ran out, even though Mrs. Connor was still talking.

I reached my bike before Ryan and Courtney got there, and I unlocked it, jumped on, and starting riding. I didn't even look back, didn't want to know if Ryan was standing there, a little disappointed that I'd ditched him or not caring in the least.

I didn't feel like going home, so instead I rode to Walgreens, where I spent a half hour looking through different colors of nail polish until finally settling on Glorious Grape, mainly because it was on clearance and I had less than three dollars on me.

When I got home, Ashley's car was in the driveway for the second day in a row, and I knew there really must be trouble in paradise. She was in her room, talking on the phone, but I walked in and sat down on the bed anyway. She shooed me away with her hand, but I pretended not to notice.

I took the Glorious Grape out of the bag and started on my left hand. I still hadn't mastered how to do the right one, and I wondered if it was something you were born knowing how to do, if it could be your genes that determined whether or not you could really make yourself look pretty. Courtney could do both hands in less than two minutes and have them look equally perfect. "Sorry"—she'd grinned when she caught me watching with my mouth open—"I'm a little ambidextrous." That's what my father would've called a million-dollar word.

Ashley said, "I have to call you back. The imp won't leave me alone." She pressed the END button. "Melissa, really. Can't you do that in your room?"

"Will you do my right hand?"

She sighed dramatically, flopped down on the bed, and rolled her eyes. "Hold out your hand."

I did, and I watched the way she wiped the brush over my thumbnail with a perfectly steady hand. Yes, clearly, her DNA had blessed her with this talent even though it had gotten lost somewhere in mine. "What's up with you and Austin?"

"Nothing's up with Austin." She glared at me.

"You don't have to be so defensive."

"Whatever." She didn't say anything for a minute. Then she said. "Talent scouts. For the minor league."

That meant nothing to me. "So?"

"So, you idiot, they're coming to watch practice this week, and I didn't want to make him nervous."

"Oh." This was the first inkling I had that Ashley actually cared about Austin in some real way, and it caught me completely by surprise. "So he might be, like, a real baseball player or something?"

"Hold still so you don't smudge them." I looked down and saw she'd finished my nails. They were perfect—bright purple in this odd grape bubblegum kind of way but clearly painted by a professional.

"Thanks," I said. "Hey, do you know who Sally Bedford is?"

She shook her head. "Why?"

"Well, no reason really. It was just someone Dad used to know. Grandma Harry said something about her."

"Oh crap," she said. "I totally forgot about her birthday. Did you?"

I shook my head. "I stopped by to see her yesterday."

"You are such a freakin' kiss-up, aren't you?" She sighed. "Go wait for them to dry in your own room, okay?" She gave me a little shove and picked up the phone again. "Go," she said. "What are you waiting for?"

◇

In my room, I thought some more about Sally Bedford, because it was better than thinking about Courtney and Ryan, together in her perfect pink bedroom, making out. Or thinking about my headache, which was throbbing more today than yesterday.

Eventually, I heard my mother come in, and I thought about going in the kitchen and asking her. But then I thought a) she knew who Sally was and would never tell me because there was something awful that I wouldn't want to hear, or b) she didn't know who Sally was and then I'd create this little shadow, this little nagging doubt in her mind that I'd created in my own, or c) she would tell me in no uncertain terms that I was hanging on to the past way too hard and way too long, and it would be much more hurtful to hear it straight from her than implied from Ryan.

So I sat there for a while, just thinking, trying to hatch a plan. And I decided that I would have to meet her face-to-face. That I would have to find her so I could ask her myself how exactly she'd known my father and my grandma Harry.

chapter *10*

There are only two seasons in the desert—summer and winter—and there never seemed to be much in between. On the last day of October the temperature was 97 degrees, and by mid-November the high was in the 60s, but the lows at night were in the 30s, so it was a chilly ride to school. I found my winter coat buried in the back of my closet and the blue gloves my mother bought me the winter we were in Philadelphia, when I'd felt real, biting cold and experienced true snow for the very first time.

I watched my breath frost the air as I rode my bike to school, alone. Because Ryan and Courtney had officially become a couple, Ryan had asked me, almost sheepishly, if I would mind if he rode his bike across the wash to Courtney's house and then walked to school with her some days. "Yeah. Whatever," I'd said. "It's a free country."

And then "some days" turned into every day, and I was stuck riding to school by myself.

In biology we were almost finished with the frog, and Mr. Finkelstein had announced that next semester, when we started on the pig, we'd be switching lab partners. I almost wanted to puke when I saw Ryan and Courtney exchange knowing glances, and Jeffrey gave me a nudge with his elbow that I pretended not to notice.

In English we were reading Oedipus, and I was stuck on the paper we were supposed to be writing about his tragic flaw. In class, Mrs. Connor gave us a hint that it had something to do with the fact that Oedipus thought he was above the gods, that he could escape a prophecy. But I really thought it was his curiosity that got him in the end. That if only he'd left well enough alone, none of the tragic stuff might have happened to him. It was this thought that made me tuck Sally Bedford away in the back of my mind for a little while. Part of me wanted to go to Charles and Large and talk to her, but it was probably too far to ride my bike there, and I hadn't gotten up the nerve to ask Ashley to drive me.

The week before Christmas break we had midterms, and the biology one on the frog was supposed to be tough. Courtney and Ryan invited me to study with them, and I accepted, mainly because I had no idea how to tell the difference between a frog liver and a frog heart and I didn't want to fail the first semester of biology.

I met them at Courtney's house the Saturday before the test.

"Meliss." Courtney hugged me when she opened the door. "It's been so long since we've hung out." She ushered me up to her bedroom, where Ryan was already stretched out on her high bed. It felt strange to see him there, all lean and long and lanky, in a position he'd been in on my bed dozens of times. But here he looked like someone else, like her Ryan. "You know what?" Courtney announced as soon as I sat down. "We need to find you a boyfriend so we can all double-date. Wouldn't that be great, Ry?"

I looked at him, but he wouldn't meet my eyes. "Yeah, sure." He didn't sound entirely convinced.

"Who do you like at school? Come on, Meliss. You can tell us."

I wasn't sure how to answer. If I said no one then she would scour the pages of Ryan's old yearbook until she found someone suitable, and if I said someone then I knew she wouldn't let up about it. "We should study," I finally said.

Paco ran into her room and started yipping, and then he sat down in my lap. I watched Ryan carefully, because I knew dogs made him wheeze. He cleared his throat a little. "Shouldn't you put Paco in the other room?" I said to Courtney.

"Why?" She looked genuinely confused, so I knew that Ryan hadn't mentioned his allergy to her. What an idiot.

"Never mind," I said. But Paco gave me a sort of curious, insulted look, as if he thought I wanted him gone. He sniffed the air a little and ran out of the room. Ryan's shoulders relaxed, and I knew he was relieved that he wasn't about to have an asthma attack in front of Courtney, or worse, that he'd have to explain to her that he didn't quite love her beloved Paco as much as he'd probably said he did.

Courtney left to get Paco some food, and Ryan came down on the floor and sat next to me. He nudged my leg with his foot. "We should have a little ceremony next week for Kermit, to celebrate his demise."

I laughed, despite the fact that I was still annoyed with him. "I think it's a little past that point, don't you?" Kermit was no longer a frog; he didn't even much resemble a *dead* frog. He was just sort of this thing now, lifeless, a specimen, so that he really could've originally been anything at all.

"But still, the poor guy deserves something, after all he's been through. Don't you think? It's not that easy being green," he started singing in the funny off-key way he has of singing everything.

"You're terrible." I started laughing again, because the truth was, Kermit wasn't even exactly green anymore, just sort of this weird rusty-brown color.

"What's so funny?" Courtney walked back in.

Ryan stopped singing. "We were just talking about poor Kermit."

She made a face. "Ugh. I can't stand it. Let's just study and get it over with already."

I agreed. The sooner we were done with this, the better.

I received a seventy-two on my frog exam, which was enough for me to earn a solid C in biology for the semester, a grade I was actually a little bit proud of, because I'd done absolute minimal dissecting and studying all fall. I got an A in Mrs. Connor's English class because she thought my take on Oedipus was original, not wrong, even though I didn't exactly go for her idea of the whole thing. I loved teachers like that, who liked it when I thought out of the box or when I disagreed with them or, as my dad always used to say, found the other silver lining, the one nobody else thought to look for. But of course, teachers like Mrs. Connor were rare at Desert Crest. I was fortunate to have ended up with her.

I got Bs in the rest of my classes, and once you averaged out the A and the C, I was a solid B student, which was more than enough to please my mother. "Very good," she'd said as she'd glanced, only barely, at my report card. And it almost felt like I was getting away with something because I knew my dad wouldn't have been satisfied, that he would've expected better from me. Before he died, I'd been a straight-A student.

chapter *11*

Just after school let out for winter break, my mom announced that Aunt Julie was coming to town for a visit. Aunt Julie never came to visit; in fact the only time she'd been here since I was born was for my dad's funeral, and even then, she and Uncle Frank were in and out in less than forty-eight hours. "Once you leave a place," my mother had said, "there's something about it that makes you never want to come back." I didn't exactly understand what she meant, and I wondered if I ever moved away if I'd want to come back here or not. Maybe I would miss the desert, all the parched and prickly landscapes and blue skies and dust and brown horizons. Or maybe

I wouldn't. Maybe if I moved somewhere on the East Coast like Aunt Julie did, I would get used to the snow in the winter and the constant sticky dewiness of the air in the spring.

Aunt Julie arrived two days before Christmas. My mom was at work and Ashley was out, so I was the only one there when she rang the doorbell. When I opened the front door, she was standing there on the front step wearing a long brown dress with her dark hair pulled back in a tight bun. She was sort of like a miniature version of my mother, only not as pretty and much more serious-looking. She wasn't wearing any makeup, and she'd gained a little weight since I'd seen her last. She had three bags, piled high on top of one another, propped up next to her. Either she didn't pack light, or she was planning on staying.

"Where's Uncle Frank?" I asked.

She cleared her throat. "It's just me this time." She stepped toward me, like she was about to hug me but wasn't sure where to put her arms, so I reached out and hugged her to avoid any awkwardness.

"Come on in." I held open the door and she pulled the suitcases through, having to fight to make it over the threshold.

I already knew that something was up. Aunt Julie did not go anywhere without Uncle Frank. Ever. Even when they came to see us when we were in Philadelphia and we were only a few hours' drive from where they lived, Aunt Julie hadn't come alone. In fact, I'd sort of made them into one person in my mind, so it felt funny to see her here by herself.

"Where is everyone?" she asked, surveying the house.

"Mom's at work and Ashley's out somewhere. Probably with her boyfriend."

"Oh." She sat down at the kitchen table and I offered her a drink. "Just some water. No ice."

I got it for her and sat down next to her.

"So your sister has a boyfriend now, huh?" I nodded. "What about you, Melissa?"

"Nope." I shook my head. My aunt and I weren't exactly what you would call close. Sure, she'd send me a card with a check for fifty dollars on my birthday, and every once in a while I'd pick up the phone and say hi or something when she called to talk to my mom, but I wasn't about to spill my guts to her or anything like that.

"I never had a boyfriend when I was your age either," she said. "Just study and keep your grades up and go to a good college. That's what really matters right now."

"Uh-huh." Clearly, Aunt Julie would've been disappointed by my report card. I could imagine her shaking her head, her tight, thin lips pursed in a frown.

"So what's it been like around here lately in the desert?"

I shrugged. I wasn't sure if she wanted a weather report or a gossip report, but I took another look at her serious, tightly woven bun and opted for the weather. "Nice," I said. "Cool. Sunny."

"Yes." She nodded. "This is always the time of year when I miss being here. Just when the snow starts to pile up in the mountains back east." She stared out the glass door into our backyard and seemed very deep in thought.

"You staying long?" I finally said, just to say something.

"Oh I don't know. A few days." She paused. "Just to catch up."

But she sounded so sad that I instantly wondered what had happened, what Uncle Frank had done.

Aunt Julie decided to take a nap, so I helped her carry her bags up to my father's old office and get the sleeper sofa all set up. "Will you wake me when your mother gets home?" she said. "I don't want to sleep till morning."

I realized I'd have the house to myself for a few more hours and I felt a little bit antsy, just itching to get out of it. I could call Ryan or Courtney, but I already knew they'd be hanging out together, and I didn't feel like playing the third wheel again.

It was a beautiful day outside, bright piercing sunshine and nearly 70 degrees, so I decided I would take a bike ride to visit Grandma Harry. I'd put "Find out more about Sally Bedford" on my mental winter-break to-do list. And if this was my tragic flaw, so be it.

I scribbled a quick note for Aunt Julie in case she woke up, grabbed my jacket, and hopped on my bike.

It turned out I was wrong about Ryan, who was in the front yard trimming a bougainvillea with this big pair of hedge cutters. "Hey there, landscaper man," I yelled.

He looked up, and I noticed a dead flower in his hair. "Hey, Mel. You riding in the wash?"

I shook my head. "To Sunset Vistas. To see my grandmother."

"Oh." We both kind of stared at each other for a minute or so.

"Wanna ride with me?" I finally said. "I could use

some company." I knew he would. Ryan was always looking for an excuse to get out of the chores his father left for him.

"Let me just go in and get my inhaler," he said.

So we rode, the two of us again. It had been nearly a month since we'd ridden at all, nearly two since we'd ridden in the wash, and I wondered if those days of treasure hunting were over, if it was something we'd finally outgrown.

"How's Courtney?" I asked him.

"She's in San Diego this week. With her dad for Christmas."

I was a little surprised that she hadn't called to tell me she was leaving. But then the other part of me, the tiny little place where I stored joy, did a momentary happy dance. I was going to have him all to myself again.

"What are you doing for Christmas?" he asked.

We hadn't really discussed it yet, beyond the fact that Aunt Julie was coming and that my mom might be inviting Kevin Baker to Christmas dinner. ("It's not a definite, girls. Only a maybe. Just a maybe." It was hard to tell if she'd meant her relationship with him or just the one dinner, but I took it that she only meant the dinner.)

"The Hair might come over," I said. "And my aunt's in town."

"You have an aunt?" he said.

It seemed strange that he didn't know that, but it's not like he ever would've met her. He and his father had come to my dad's funeral, but we weren't going around making tons of introductions or anything. "Yeah. My mom's sister. She lives in Pennsylvania."

"Wow." He shook his head. "I totally did not know that about you. What do you call her?"

"Aunt Julie."

"No, I mean like a nickname."

"Oh." I hadn't really thought about it before; she wasn't exactly a big-enough part of my life to warrant it.

"What does she do?"

"She's a sociology professor."

"Perfect. The Professor."

I nodded. That suited her, stodgy and serious, but I felt a little bad thinking about how sad she'd been earlier, so I added, "She's really not so bad," though I had no idea if this was completely true or not.

"Man." He shook his head. "I can't believe your mom's still dating the Hair. That's insane."

"I know," I said, but I didn't want to say anything

else, didn't even want to talk about him because the more I thought or talked about him, the more real he felt. And the more real he felt, the sadder I got about my father all over again.

We pulled into the Sunset Vistas parking lot and stopped our bikes by the front doors. "You wanna come in?" I asked. Ryan had met Grandma Harry before, when we were younger, but he hadn't seen her in years, not since she'd become infinitely forgetful.

"Naw," he said. "I'll wait for you out here. Guard the bikes, in case any old fart tries to escape."

"You're terrible," I said, but I was still smiling.

Grandma Harry was sitting up in bed watching *Oprah*, or she had *Oprah* on and she was staring at the TV anyway. "Oh, Melissa." She waved me in. "Honey pie. I was just thinking about you."

"You were?"

"This lady on *Oprah* holds the record for reading the most books in the entire world, and I was just thinking about how you always used to read so much, and your father would help you keep a list of all the books you read."

Yes. So long ago. In a world before Dr. Singh and cancer and death, I had been a serious and avid reader, a frequent checker-outer at the library. It was a part of my life I'd forgotten about until that moment, until she'd gone and given it back to me, like a gift. "How many books has she read?" I asked, pointing to the TV.

"Oh I don't know, honey pie. Dang it, I can't remember. Maybe a million. Oh my memory is terrible. Come sit down and watch with me."

I pulled up a chair, but I wasn't really interested in watching. I'd come here on a mission. Sally Bedford. Sally Bedford. Sally Bedford. And I didn't want to leave Ryan waiting outside too long. So I just decided to blurt it out. "Grandma," I said.

"What, honey pie?"

"Can I ask you something about my dad?"

She turned her eyes from the TV to me, and her eyes looked way too deep and intense for the eyes of a person who was half missing behind them. "He's dead. Isn't he?" she said.

It was a relief to hear her say it, to hear her remember, to not have to dance around the obvious, make up an excuse, or lie. I nodded. "Yes," I said. "He is."

"How did it happen? How did he die?"

"Cancer," I said.

"My memory is terrible." She shook her head. "My

memory is just so bad." She reached for my hand, and when I gave it to her, she squeezed it.

"A few months ago when I was here, I asked you about Dad's old girlfriends, and you said something about Sally Bedford. Who was she?"

"Oh, honey pie"—she let go of my hand and leaned it on her forehead as if she had developed a terrible migraine—"did I really say that?"

I nodded.

"You know my memory is terrible. I can't remember saying that."

"I know," I said. "It's okay. We all forget things." It was a lame attempt to make her feel better and I knew it, but there were only so many times I could nod and smile when she told me how forgetful she was before I felt the need to try to make her feel better. "But Grandma, who was she? How did Dad know her?"

She grabbed my hand again, and she squeezed it really tight. "Honey pie, sometimes it's better to forget."

Ryan was lying on a half wall next to our bikes, sunning himself when I walked out. He had his sunglasses on, so it was hard to tell if he was napping or daydreaming. "Hey, get up." I pushed his leg a little bit, and he sat up.

"Are you up for a ride?"

"Well, duh. I'm here aren't I?"

"No, I mean a real ride. I'm going to Charles and Large."

"Mel, you can't be serious."

"What?" I shrugged. It couldn't be more than another five miles or so to Charles and Large, and we'd already come this far. We could do it. I thought briefly about my aunt Julie napping in my father's study and the fact that my mother might beat me home, but then I pushed those thoughts aside. I was going to find Sally, and I was going to find her today.

He sighed and hopped back on his bike. "What is so damn important at Charles and Large?"

"I'll tell you once I figure it out," I said.

So we pedaled across flat and gridded streets until we got closer to the center of town. I kept pedaling even when my legs were tired, even when I heard Ryan's breathing, thick and heavy behind me, but I stopped when he stopped, when he pulled out the inhaler and sucked on it, hard. "We're almost there," I said.

"Mel, I don't think I can do it." His voice sounded raspy.

"You can."

"But I'll never make it home."

"We'll call Ashley to pick us up and we'll come back for our bikes in the morning." I was inventing a plan on the spot, not really thinking it through enough to realize that Ashley might not come for us, that she might not even answer if we called her. But I kept pedaling. Because I had to, because I needed to know.

And then at last I saw it there, over the horizon, the big Charles and Large sign with the logo that reminded me of a Christmas-tree star, sitting right there against the backdrop of a purple-and-brown mountain, as if it were native to the desert, as if it belonged here.

"It looks pretty empty," Ryan said, wheezing. He was referring to the parking lot, which had only maybe ten cars left in it. And it occurred to me that it was almost Christmas, that everyone was probably on vacation.

I left my bike by the front entrance, not even bothering to chain it, and Ryan did the same. He followed me inside without saying anything else, maybe because he thought I was acting a little crazy or maybe because he was just entirely out of breath. I'd taken it all from him, everything he had.

The front receptionist was still at her desk. She was

a large woman in a sacky black dress, and she wore her phone in a headset and typed something on her computer while she talked. I sat in a chair and waited until she hung up.

"Can I help you?" She stared at me kind of funny, turning her head to the side. "Do I know you?"

"No," I said, but then I realized that maybe she did, because she looked vaguely familiar, and she might've worked here when my dad did, she might've been at his funeral. Who could really be sure? His work friends, his companions had all just been a blur, a sea of stretched and unfamiliar faces. I cleared my throat. "I'm looking for Sally Bedford."

"Oh, well, you're about six months too late." I immediately jumped to the conclusion that she was dead, which simultaneously annoyed me and made me feel somewhat relieved. I was never going to know the truth. "She hasn't worked here since June," she said. Not dead. Just fired. Or she quit.

"But she was on your website. I saw her picture."

She laughed. "She was the one who did our website, and the big guys"—she pointed in the direction of what I assumed to be Charles's or Large's office—"have come down hard on the budget. So they haven't rehired for her position yet."

"Do you know where she works now?"

"I have no idea." She squinted. "You related to her or something? I know I know you from somewhere."

"Not quite," I said. "Thank you for your time."

I grabbed Ryan's arm and pulled him toward the door. "McAllister," I heard her say behind me. "That's it. Yes, Tim, or was it Tom?"

I quickly tried to wipe away the tears that sprang into my eyes before Ryan could notice them.

From the parking lot, I called Ashley's cell three times before she picked up. "What's your problem?" she yelled into the phone when she finally answered. She was breathing heavily, and it occurred to me that maybe she and Austin had been in the middle of making out. The thought that she was lying there half naked with him or something really creeped me out. It's just not the way I wanted to think of her.

"I need you to pick me up," I said.

"No."

"Seriously, Ash. I really need a favor. Just this once."

"You're a big girl, Melissa. Just find another ride, all right? Or call Mom."

"But I—" She hung up on me before I had a chance to finish. "Bitch," I whispered to no one in particular, though Ryan heard me.

"Oh crap. She's not coming, is she?"

I shook my head. "I'll call my mom." Really, it was the absolute last thing I wanted to do, because there was no possible way I was going to explain it to her where it would make any sense. Maybe this was my tragic flaw, not thinking things through. "You have to dive with your head, Melon, not your heart," my father always used to tell me when I was younger and I'd get in trouble for doing something stupid that I hadn't really thought about first. Whereas my mother just never had the patience and would say something like, "Oh honestly, Melissa. What were you thinking?"

Then I remembered: Aunt Julie. The Professor. I didn't really know her, and she didn't really owe me anything, but I had a feeling she would hop in the shiny blue rental car I'd seen in the driveway on my way out and come get us.

"My dad is going to kill me," Ryan said.

Mr. Thomason was a tall and serious-looking man whom I rarely ever saw smile, and there was something about him that always scared me just a little bit. "I'm going to call my aunt," I said. I dialed my home number; it rang five times and I got the voice mail. So I called back two more times, until she finally picked up. "McAllister residence," she said in this short and formal way that sounded nothing like how any of us ever would've answered the phone.

"It's me," I said. "Melissa."

"Your mom's not back yet, and neither is Ashley."

"I know." I paused, considering how to ask her. "Can you come pick me up?"

"Pick you up? Where are you?"

I told her.

"Okay," she said. And she hung up. No argument. No questions.

While we waited, Ryan and I sat on the ground next to our bikes in silence for a few minutes. His breathing had slowed back to normal, but his face was still red and flushed. "You mad?" I finally said.

He shook his head. "Well," he said, "maybe a little." He paused. "What are you doing here anyway? What's with this whole Sally Bedford thing?"

"She's someone my dad knew."

He frowned. "Knew how?"

I shrugged. "I don't know. That's what I'm trying to find out."

"Mel . . ."

"What?"

"Nothing. Just forget it."

"No," I said, suddenly on the verge of crying. "Just say it. I'm crazy. This is ridiculous." I sucked in my breath a little bit and willed myself not to cry. "I'm sorry, but I am not perfect, like Courtney. I'm not beautiful. I worry about things. I didn't get a new dog and a pink bedroom to help me forget." That last part was mean and I knew it, but still, I didn't feel like apologizing.

He was quiet and looking down at his shoes, and when he finally said something, it was barely louder than a whisper. "I was just going to say that you might find something out that you don't want to know, ya know?"

I knew he was thinking about his mother and the gardener, because that's the way Ryan sometimes saw the world: all black or white or good or bad.

"I know," I said.

He looked at me. "I can help you if you want. But I just don't want you to get hurt." He put his arm around me and pulled me toward him in a sort of half hug, and despite the fact that we were both sweating, I wanted to lean into him, wanted to let him hold on to me.

"I'm sorry," I said.

"You are crazy."

"Shut up." I elbowed him and he laughed. "Don't tell Courtney though, okay? I just don't want her to make this into some whole big thing."

At the mention of Courtney he pulled his arm away and stood a little farther away from me. "Okay," he said. "Our secret."

My aunt didn't say anything until after we dropped Ryan off at his house. "That your boyfriend?" she said.

"No. I told you. I don't have a boyfriend. Just a boy. Just a friend."

She nodded. "Sure. I had one of those when I was your age. Frank."

"You were friends with Uncle Frank when you were in high school?"

"I was hopelessly in love with him." She laughed. "But I think he always wanted to date your mother. Of course, everyone always wanted to date your mother." She laughed again, but she didn't sound bitter, not the way I sometimes felt about everyone thinking Ashley was beautiful and thinking I was an imp.

"Well, that's not the way it is with me and Ryan," I said. "I mean I'm not hopelessly in love with him or anything."

"Okay."

"Really. And besides, he has a girlfriend."

She nodded. "I believe you."

"Good."

She parked the car in the driveway; I got my bike out of the trunk and we went in.

My mother was sitting in the kitchen. "Oh, you two. There you are. I couldn't imagine where you'd gone." She was waiting for an answer, but neither one of us gave it to her. "Well, never mind," she finally said. She wrapped Aunt Julie up in a big hug. "Oh, Jules, it's so good to see you. How was your flight?" But she didn't give Aunt Julie much chance to answer before she said, "Melissa, sweetie, where's your sister?"

I shrugged. If she thought I actually kept track of Ashley's social life then she'd definitely lost her grip on reality. And I knew that wherever Ashley was, she didn't want to be bothered.

"We'll call her from the car."

"Where are we going?"

"Kevin's meeting us for dinner."

I sucked my breath in a little bit. My mom didn't seem to notice, but Aunt Julie caught my eye. "Oh, Cyn. I'm exhausted."

My mother sighed. "I really want you to meet him and he's going to LA tomorrow for the holidays." I wondered briefly what was in LA and if there was some small chance that he might forget all about my mother and decide to stay there. "Please. We'll make it short."

"Can I take a shower?" I asked. The sweat from my bike ride had dried, but I felt disgusting and my hair was a mess.

"You look fine, Melissa." She didn't even look at me as she said it. "Just go put on something nice and meet me in the garage in five minutes. I'm going to go call your sister."

I knew my mother's opinion of something nice and mine were two different things. But I decided to go with mine. I put on a pair of dark-wash jeans, a black sweater, and my black flip-flops. And then I took the rainbow piece of glass out of the jewelry case on my dresser, held it in my hand for a minute, and slipped it into my pocket.

I'm not sure what my mom said to Ashley, but by the time we arrived at the restaurant, she was already waiting for us there in the parking lot, all smiles.

"Where were you, sweetie?" My mom kissed her on the cheek.

She got out of answering by giving Aunt Julie a big enthusiastic hug. "Hey, Aunt Julie." I smiled to myself, thinking that Ashley had a secret too, that I wasn't the only one doing something my mother wouldn't be happy about.

"Well, come on, girls. Let's go inside." I could tell my mother was nervous because she was chewing on the edge of the skin by her thumb, something she did only when she was feeling stressed. When we were in Philadelphia for my dad's treatment, she chewed on it so much that her thumb started bleeding.

I was not happy about seeing Kevin, and I suddenly felt exhausted from the long bike ride. My legs were thick and Jell-O-ey and aching, and my head was starting to hurt. "You look like crap," Ashley whispered to me as we were walking in. "Where were you when you called me?"

I ignored her and pushed past her so I got to walk in first behind my mother. As someone who'd hung up on me in my time of need, she didn't deserve to know.

After I pushed in front of Ashley, I saw him there,

sitting at a table by the edge of the restaurant: Kevin Baker. More gorgeous, handsome, and tan than he'd looked that first night at our house when he came to pick my mom up. And yes, now that I could see him up close, definitely younger than she was.

He stood up, waved to all of us, and then walked up to my mom and gave her a quick hug and kiss on the cheek.

"Kevin, this is my sister, Julie," my mom said.

"Nice to meet you," he said. He pulled out my mother's chair for her, helped her push it in, and then left his hand on her shoulder for a moment. She turned and looked back at him and smiled, and it was so obvious that she was taken with him. I thought I was going to throw up.

We all sat down and looked at the menu for a while, and nobody said much, until Kevin chimed in with, "What's everyone going to order?"

"Well," my Aunt Julie said, "they don't have much choice for vegans here, do they?"

"You're vegan?" my mom said. Aunt Julie nodded. "For how long?"

"Five, no, six years now."

My mother shook her head. "How didn't I know this

about you? I would've picked a different place. There's a great little salad place next to the salon."

"I'm sure I told you. It's just—" She stopped, but we all knew what she was thinking, that she'd told my mother at a time when there'd been too many other things to think about, illnesses and treatments to consume her, and I was guessing this was not a period of time she ever discussed with Kevin. "Well, don't worry about it, Cyn," my aunt said. "I'm not that hungry anyway."

"Neither am I," Ashley chimed in. I rolled my eyes at no one in particular. Aunt Julie had been trying to spare my mother's feelings, but Ashley was probably getting herself ready for another beauty pageant. Spring was her season, and it was just around the corner.

I, on the other hand, was starving, and I was planning to eat. A lot. Like a carnivore. So I ordered a steak and mashed potatoes and soup and a milk shake. "My goodness," Kevin said. "It's nice to see a girl with a good appetite." His voice was annoying, kind of deep and scratchy, almost like he was trying to be some TV cowboy or something.

"She's such a pig," Ashley said.

"Whatever. And you're totally anorexic," I spat back at her.

"Girls, please." My mother's voice sounded tight, strained, so I kept my mouth shut, but I stuck my tongue out at Ashley when my mother turned back to face Kevin. *Bitch*, she mouthed to me silently. "Girls, did I tell you Kevin owns a ranch? With horses and everything."

She hadn't. In fact, she'd barely told us anything about Kevin except for when she was going out with him and maybe where they were going. Why she thought we'd be impressed by horses, though, I'm not sure. Ashley and I couldn't have cared less. But Ashley, always the kiss-up said, "Oooh. Horses. That's cool."

"You girls ride?" Kevin asked, more to her than to me.

I chewed on a piece of bread for a minute while she said, "No. No. I never have."

Then, for some reason, what I said next just popped out of my mouth. "Mom did. Didn't you?"

Kevin looked surprised.

"Didn't she ever tell you about the time she was Queen of the Rodeo and she had to ride a horse in her pageant dress?"

"Oh, sweetie, that was so long ago." My mother's face was turning red, and I could tell I was embarrassing her, but I didn't stop.

"That was the summer you met Dad. Wasn't it?"

"Oh yes. It was." Aunt Julie laughed. "You hated that damn horse, Cyn." She held her hand over her mouth after she said it, as if realizing maybe she shouldn't have, that she was giving away some secret about my mother. "That was a long time ago though. Wasn't it?"

"Yes." My mother glared at her the same way Ashley and I usually glared at each other, and it was amusing to see it, my mother getting annoyed at her sister. "It was a long time ago."

Kevin laughed. "Well, if any of you girls want to learn to ride, I'm a great teacher." None of us said anything. We were not the horse-riding kind of people and we all knew it, even my mother. "Maybe you, Julie, before you go back East."

"Oh no. I couldn't. I'm too old to learn now."

"The girls would enjoy learning to ride. Wouldn't you, girls?" My mother glared at us as she said it, as if to say, You'd better say yes or else.

I grabbed another piece of bread and started stuffing it in my mouth. Ashley made a face at me. "Can you stop inhaling your carbs? It's making me sick."

"I'm going to use the little girls' room before the food gets here. Anyone else?" Aunt Julie said. I smiled at her, grateful, and Ashley jumped out of her chair.

◇

The three of us walked to the back of the restaurant, toward the restrooms, though I was pretty sure that none of us had to go. "Do you mind if I go outside to have a smoke, girls?" my aunt asked, which shocked me, because I had no idea that she smoked and she just didn't seem like the type. A vegan who was also a smoker? That seemed like a total contradiction to me, but I decided I wouldn't question it as long as it was getting me away from the table.

"Can I come outside with you?" Ashley said, and I nodded in agreement.

"Okay, but don't tell your mother that I smoke. Or that I let you watch me. And don't ever smoke, girls. It's a terrible, terrible habit. I swear it." We nodded and watched her shaking hands fumble in her purse for a cigarette. "So what do you think of the cowboy?" She chuckled as if she knew some sort of inside joke that we didn't.

"He's okay," Ashley said.

"I am not learning to ride a horse," I announced, as if it were the craziest and most barbaric idea in the world.

"Well, neither am I," Ashley huffed.

My aunt inhaled on her cigarette deeply, then exhaled, a white puff of smoke clouding up around our heads. "I know it's tough. But you should give him a chance. It means a lot to her." She took another drag on the cigarette. "After our father died, your mother and I hated every guy that our mother brought home, and then she ended up dying all alone." Her voice trailed off, and she looked off toward the sky, toward the rolling evening clouds.

My mother never ever talked about her own parents; all Ashley and I knew was that they were dead, and that they'd been that way since before we were born. I never knew that her father had died first or that her mother had been lonely, and in a way it made me feel a sadness for my mother that I hadn't ever thought to feel before. "How did your father die?" I asked her.

"Melissa." Ashley nudged me.

"No. It's okay. Doesn't your mother ever talk about it?" We shook our heads. "Well, she was older than me, so she would remember more. You should ask her sometime. He had a heart attack. It was all very quick. One day he was there, and the next day he wasn't. I was eight."

I wondered how things would've been different for us if my dad had died suddenly rather than slowly, if it would've made things better or worse. I wasn't sure.

My aunt threw her cigarette to the ground and crushed it with her foot. She took some sweet floral-smelling perfume out of her purse and sprayed it on all of us. "We should go back in. Your mother will think we've fallen into the toilet."

"Aunt Julie," Ashley said, "thanks."

She put an arm around each one of us and gave us both a hug at the same time. "You two have each other. And don't you forget it. No matter what. You hold on to that."

chapter 12

Just after Christmas, Aunt Julie announced she was going to stay a whole other week and a half, until the end of our break. "Are you sure?" My mother looked at her through narrowed eyes, so I knew she knew something that Ashley and I didn't.

"Yes," my aunt said. "It does me good to be back here."

"Well, Kevin was serious about those lessons." Though I barely knew her, I knew that there was no way in hell Julie was getting on a horse, but all she said to my mother was, "We'll see how it goes, Cyn."

I didn't see Ryan again over break. As soon as Christmas was over, Courtney came back, and Ryan and his father left to visit his grandmother in Texas.

Courtney called to ask me if I'd seen him. "I saw him the other day," I said, leaving out all the details about our horrible bike ride. "He's in Texas now."

"Oh." She sounded both surprised and annoyed, and it made me just a little bit happy to know that he hadn't told her he was leaving.

"I'm sure he meant to tell you," I said. "He always goes to Texas for New Year's."

"Well, that's cool." She sighed. "Okay. I'm totally bored now. We should hang out."

I felt a little bit like a yo-yo, bouncing aimlessly back and forth between the two of them, but only when they wanted me to, only when they weren't together. "I don't know," I lied. "I'm kinda busy. My aunt's in town."

"Oh come on, Meliss. Just come over and hang out for a little while."

And I said yes. Because there was something about her that was utterly irresistible, that sucked me in and wouldn't let go, and in a way, I could understand why Ryan was dating her.

So I hopped on my bike and rode across the wash. It was the first day I'd ridden since my long ride to Charles and

Large, and as soon as my feet spun the pedals I felt the aches in my calves, the muscles protesting being put back in use.

The first thing I noticed about Courtney was that she was incredibly tan, and I wondered if it was real or fake. I decided on fake because it had sort of an orangy glow to it at first, but in the light of her bedroom it looked entirely real, and her skin reminded me of a perfectly toasted marshmallow.

"How was San Diego?" I asked.

"Oh." She sighed. "It was unbelievably fabulous."

"That's good."

She stretched out on the floor and Paco jumped up on her stomach. I sat down next to her and started flipping through a fashion magazine, noticing how all the girls were even skinnier than Ashley and much taller, too, and they were wearing this dramatic eye makeup that I guessed would look clownlike on me.

"Meliss, can you keep a secret?" she asked.

I looked up. I nodded, but deep down I was thinking, well, it depended what kind of secret and who she wanted me to keep it from, though it seemed obvious that it would be Ryan.

"Mark and I made out on the beach."

"Mark, the one who always grabbed your boobs?" I asked, incredulous. She giggled and I had this mental image of this big, muscular lifeguard-ish guy pushing his hands up under her shirt.

"It was just a one-time thing. For old times' sake."

"Why are you telling me?" Because it hit me, all at once, this crushing enormous weight that she'd just thrown on my chest, the burden of knowing something that I didn't want to know and having to keep it to myself.

"Well, we're friends, aren't we?"

I nodded, but I was feeling a little skeptical.

"And besides. It was stupid. It didn't mean anything." She paused. "And we totally already dated before, so it doesn't even count."

I knew that it would count to Ryan. Ryan, who'd doubted people's intentions since his mother ran off with the gardener; Ryan, who was supposedly my best friend; Ryan. "You know." I stood up. "I'm sorry. I have to go."

"But you just got here."

"I have to meet my aunt," I lied.

"Meliss, you won't say anything, will you?"

I thought for a moment and then shook my head.

"No. Of course not," I said, but I hadn't yet decided if I would or not.

It was only a half lie that I was meeting my aunt, because she was there at the house when I got back, and so was Ashley. "We were waiting for you," Aunt Julie said when I came in.

"For me?"

"Come on. I'm going to take you girls on a drive."

We all hopped into Aunt Julie's rental car, Ashley up front and me in the back, because that's the way it always was. She was older, so she got to ride shotgun when there were three of us going anywhere. Aunt Julie rolled the window down and smoked, her hand hanging carelessly out of the car with the cigarette attached. She looked nothing like a professor; my image of her had always been all wrong, and Ryan's nickname didn't suit her at all.

Neither Ashley nor I asked where we were going, which was kind of strange, but since that night at the restaurant we both decided that we liked our aunt, that she was someone we could trust.

We drove for about ten minutes, then turned down a residential street of older, almost historic-looking houses. The houses had trees so large in the front yards that they created a pool of shade in the sunny street, and the houses had almost a more East Coast Victorian look to them than the ones in our neighborhood.

Aunt Julie pulled up in front of a house and stopped. "Okay," she said. "We're here."

"Where?" Ashley asked, and I nodded, though neither one of them was looking at me.

"You've never been here before, girls?" We shook our heads. "This is where your mother and I grew up."

The house looked pleasant enough, though small and a bit overgrown with shrubs in the front. I tried to imagine my mother and Aunt Julie as kids, running around out front here, but the image didn't come easily.

There was something about seeing a place out of my mother's past that astounded me, that made me feel sad for her and annoyed with her all at once. Because I wished she'd shown us herself, before. "I lived here until I went to college," Aunt Julie said. "And the first year when I was away, my mother died, and I never came back." She paused, as if remembering something about the house that struck her as sort of odd. "Your mother was pregnant with you, Ashley, and at the end our mother was very sick. That's why I went so far away to go to college.

To get away from her. I'm not good at taking care of people." She paused. "But your mother, she'd come over here three, four times a day with groceries and stories and cleaning supplies." She let her voice trail off, as if the memory were so clear to her she could almost taste it in a way.

"Why are you telling us all this?" Ashley finally said.

"Because," she said. "It's good to know what kind of person your mother is."

It did not seem right that you could be both a beautiful person and a good person. In my head, they'd always been separate. My mother was clearly beautiful, as was Ashley. But my dad and me, we were the good ones.

I tried to picture my mother, pregnant and swollen and waddling around in the fiery desert summer with bags of groceries for her sick mother. It was a strange image, because I'd never really thought about her that way before, which seemed sort of dumb because she never complained about taking care of my father or helping Grandma Harry.

I went into Ashley's room after Aunt Julie and my mother had both gone to bed. She was lying on her bed, reading a book on beauty pageants my mother had bought her. I plopped down on the bed next to her. Neither of us said anything for a few minutes, and then Ashley finally said, "We could learn to ride horses."

I made a face, but deep down I knew she was right. "I will if you will," I finally said.

"We just won't tell anyone at school."

I nodded, wondering if Mr. September would care if my sister hung out with a cowboy and started smelling like horse poop. "And we'll just go one time. Just one lesson."

"One lesson," she repeated. "That's all."

chapter *13*

The day school started up again, Aunt Julie, true to her word, stuffed her three suitcases into her rental car and drove herself to the airport.

"Oh I wish you would stay longer, Jules." My mother held on to her tightly, and they rocked each other back and forth, in the driveway, almost in a dance. "You'll come back again, won't you?"

"Of course," she said, but it was hard to tell if she really would or not.

I, for one, was going to miss her, and I guessed Ashley might too. It was nice to have her around the house and to have her to talk to. She wrote her phone number down on a scrap of paper and handed it to me before she left. "If you ever want to talk," she said, "I'm only a phone call away." She also promised to email us, but I didn't think it would be the same.

So I was feeling a little sad as I rode my bike to school, alone. Ryan wasn't waiting for me, and I figured he'd gone ahead and met Courtney, and of course Ashley had to pick up Mr. September.

I got to school a little early, and as I was chaining up my bike, I heard someone calling my name. I didn't recognize the voice at first, so I was surprised when I looked up and saw Max Healy standing right there, right in front of me. "Hey," I said, trying to sound nonchalant, but my heart was pounding hard in my chest.

"How was your break?"

"It was okay." I shrugged, trying to act cool, and I willed myself to think of something funny or smart to say. But nothing came to me. Finally, I said, "How was your break?"

"Not bad." He smiled. "Hey, a bunch of us are going to Jackson's after school, if you want to come." Jackson's was this restaurant right down the road from Desert Crest High where they served pizza and ice cream and a lot of the popular kids went to hang out. I'd only been there one time, when I was much younger, with my parents, after Ashley was in a play and we'd gone over afterward to get some ice cream.

"Seriously?" I said, which was an incredibly stupid thing to say, but it was what popped out. I was immediately cynical. Why would Max be inviting me?

He smiled and started walking up the steps to the school, and after the first few his walk turned into a run. When he got to the top he turned back and waved.

I was in such a daze that I didn't notice that Ryan and Courtney had arrived until they were standing right in front of me. "Were you talking to Max?" Courtney asked, her voice thick with disbelief.

"Yeah." I nodded.

"You're friends with him now?" Ryan said.

"Well, why not?" I snapped. "Why do you care?"

"I don't know," Ryan said. "Guys like him are jerks."

"Guys like him? What does that mean, anyway?" I picked up my school bag and started up the steps, breaking into a run halfway up, just the way Max had.

All day I debated whether or not I was really going to go to Jackson's after school. Maybe Max had been kidding. Maybe it was all some big practical joke, and when

I showed up, everyone would start laughing and pointing and saying, Oh my God, look, it's the imp. Or maybe not. Maybe he actually liked me.

I thought about it all through biology, as we picked our partners for the pig and I got stuck with Jeffrey. "Don't worry, Meliss," Courtney said as she clung to Ryan's arm. "Nothing's going to change. We'll all still work at the same lab table." Jeffrey rolled his eyes at me, but I pretended not to notice.

I even thought about it in English, tuning out Mrs. Connor as she talked about how we would spend the second half of the year entirely on poetry. Ugh.

When the bell rang, I jumped out of my seat, even though Mrs. Connor was in the middle of a sentence and most of the other people in the class stayed seated and let her finish.

As I walked outside, I saw Ashley and the Nose standing on the front steps, talking to Austin and some of his friends. Ashley looked right at me as I walked by, then quickly looked away. "Ashley," I whispered, trying to get her to look at me with some recognition. "Ashley." Nothing. "Ashley McAllister." I said it loud enough so the group of them stopped talking. They turned and looked at me; the Nose giggled.

Ashley pushed her way through the bunch of them. "What?" she said through gritted teeth.

I pulled her away from her crowd a little bit so they weren't all listening to me. "Max invited me to come to Jackson's after school. Should I go? I don't know what to do." I was looking for some sisterly advice, though why I expected her to give me some, I couldn't exactly say.

"Max. Max Healy?" The surprise in her voice was enough to make me smile. I nodded. Then she recovered. "Well, he was probably just trying to be nice. He probably felt bad for you or something. You totally look like a homeless girl in that outfit." She was referring to the old worn-in jeans and the college sweatshirt that used to belong to my dad. "You know he likes Lexie, and she likes him."

No, I didn't know that Lexie, "the Nose," had a thing for Max. But then, who didn't? And I certainly hadn't known that he liked her. "So?" I finally said.

"So do whatever you want," she said. "But just don't get all crazy in love with him or anything."

Austin walked over and put a hand on Ashley's shoulder. "You ready?" He kissed the back of her neck in a way that made her giggle and gave me the creeps. And I decided that I wasn't going to go. But then I turned toward the bike rack and saw Ryan and Courtney, leaning against the wall, their lips locked in a passionate kiss. I was going.

I decided to walk so I wouldn't have to extricate my bike from the lovebirds, and besides, Jackson's wasn't far. Other people walked there in groups, with friends and boyfriends, but I went alone, just me, and I hoped Max would even remember that he'd invited me.

The front wall of Jackson's was a huge glass window, and I stood there on the outside, looking through it, watching. Max was sitting at a table with a bunch of other guys I'd seen around school but didn't really know that well. They were laughing, having a good time.

I heard Ashley's giggle, and I looked up and saw her and Austin and the Nose run through the door. "Hey, Max," I heard the Nose say.

I didn't wait around to see what happened next. I walked back toward school to get my bike and ride home.

My Parents: Part II

After Tom had his appendix out, he didn't see Cynthia
again for six months. In fact, he probably would've never seen

her again. He'd lost the napkin with her number on it that Harriet had given him, and then he'd gone back to school, started dating a sorority girl (maybe Sally Bedford?) and forgotten all about her.

Harriet did not forget. She kept the idea of Cynthia tucked quietly in the back of her head. One day, when Harriet was in town visiting her son, she happened to pick up a copy of the local newspaper at breakfast, and there, as if in answer to her prayers, was a picture of Cynthia Howard sitting on top of a horse wearing a tiara. "Oh my good Lord," Harriet muttered to herself. "Would you look at that?"

Harriet took it as a sign. She took out the phone book, called all fourteen local listings for "Howard" until Cynthia herself answered the phone, on Harriet's very last try. After reintroducing herself, Harriet said, "Well, congratulations on your crown, dear."

"Oh." Cynthia was embarrassed. She knew it was a start but not the big time. Not Miss Arizona or Miss America.

"Let me buy you lunch," Harriet told her. "You were so kind to me at the hospital."

"Oh no. You don't have to," Cynthia said. "It's really not necessary."

"Please," Harriet said. "I want to."

Cynthia agreed.

The next day, she went to the restaurant. She looked around the room for Harriet's poofy blond curls, and as she was looking she caught Tom's eye. He was sitting at a table by the window, all alone.

She waved and walked toward him. "Hi there," he said.

"I was supposed to be meeting your mother."

He laughed. "So was I."

Harriet was tucked away in her little white car, already halfway back to Scottsdale.

chapter *14*

Now that Aunt Julie was gone and Ryan and Courtney were back to ignoring me again, I started to think about how else I was going to search for Sally. Ryan hadn't mentioned anything to me about it since the day we'd gone on our long bike ride, and it seemed like his offer to help hadn't been a real offer at all.

After school I'd lie on my bed and read through my father's journal, looking for anything, for a hint of the person he might've or could've been. I learned that clinophobia is the fear of going to bed, something I certainly didn't have as I seemed to be spending an extraordinary amount of time in mine lately. And I also learned that your ribs move five million times a year, every time you breathe in and out. This one kind of creeped me out, and I became superaware of my own breathing, so much that I started to feel this pain, this tightness pulling on my chest every time I inhaled and exhaled. I wondered if that's what it felt like to Ryan every time he had an asthma attack.

But there was nothing else I could find in his journal, save that one little scrap of paper with Sally Bedford's name on it. So I figured that meant that a) she wasn't really that important at all, despite what Grandma Harry said, or b) whatever it was about her that made her so important must've happened after my dad got sick and he pretty much stopped recording things in the journal.

I had no idea if she lived close still or if she'd moved, or if she was even still alive. It happened, all the time, every day. People got sick. People died. People crashed their cars and shattered themselves and broke. People did not have the life of glass.

But then, one afternoon, I flipped through my own journal, through my parents' love story, and the part about my grandma Harry finding my mother by looking in the phone book caught my eye. It occurred to me that maybe I could just look Sally up that way, in the online white pages. As easy as that. Why hadn't I thought about it before?

I went to my computer and I felt my heart pounding furiously as I typed her name in. Three seconds later, one entry came up, only one Sally Bedford in our town. But there was no information with it. It simply said *unlisted*, a word that brought tears to my eyes.

Just before Valentine's Day, Ashley and I had our first horse-riding lesson with Kevin. My mother had been so excited when Ashley told her we wanted to do it that she'd jumped up and down and clapped her hands together.

"We're only doing one lesson," I said.

"Oh, girls, you don't know how important it is for me that you get to know Kevin."

Ashley shot me a look. We hadn't realized it was *that* important to her. When she put it like that, it sounded like she was ready to marry the guy or something. So it was an understatement to say I was not excited on the drive over to his ranch.

Ashley didn't seem thrilled about it either. She wasn't being mean to me, but she wasn't saying much of anything. She didn't even complain about missing out on a Saturday afternoon with Mr. September. When we were almost there, she started to say something. Then changed her mind and stopped.

"What?" I said, glad that she was going to start a conversation because the silence hurt my head, made me feel heavy and dull and guilty and annoyed all at once.

"You know that Dad hated horses."

I shook my head. No. I hadn't known that. And it seemed so unfair that Ashley knew so much more about our father than I did, that just those two extra years made her old enough to remember little important things that I would never be able to get back now.

"Yeah, one time he took me to the rodeo parade."

"Where was I?"

She shrugged. "I don't know. I think you were sick or something and Mom stayed home with you." I had absolutely no recollection of any of this, but I knew for sure I'd never been to the rodeo parade. My dad had always made fun of the fact that we lived in a city that gave us two days off school for Rodeo in February and had some giant parade to celebrate it. "We were just standing there watching the parade, and there were all these floats and people on horses wearing cowboy hats. And then this little kid's horse got spooked, and the horse shot up in the air and threw him. It was so freaky. I mean this kid was just flying through the air until he hit the pavement."

I shuddered. "What happened to him?"

"I don't know," she said. "I don't remember. I just remember Dad cursing and talking about how horses are such dangerous animals."

"Well, now I really want to go get on a horse." I didn't think Ashley had been trying to scare me half to death, but she'd gone and done it anyway. I hadn't thought about the fact that these lessons with Kevin were going to be dangerous—annoying, yes, but I hadn't been thinking that the horse could throw me or trample me or kill me.

"I'm sure Kevin knows what he's doing," she said, but she didn't sound entirely convinced herself.

Kevin's ranch was large and sprawling, with dusty fenced-in enclosures and an L-shaped brick house that sat at the end of a long driveway. DUSTY MEADOWS, the sign by the driveway read. "Lame." Ashley shook her head when she read it. For once, we were both in agreement.

I wondered—if my mother and Kevin ever did get married—if we would have to move here. Though it was only fifteen minutes away from our neighborhood, it felt like it was in nowheresville, the middle of the desert, all dirt and cactus and sagebrush, and horses that roamed behind a wooden fence looking sort of annoyed.

I thought about the fact that Aunt Julie had left this city for college and never returned, and I knew immediately that if this was the place I had to come home to, I would not be coming back either. This would never be my home.

Kevin was waiting for us, standing on his front porch in some weird cowboy-ish attire, complete with black leather boots and a black cowboy hat. "God," Ashley muttered. "He looks like a bad country singer or something."

She was right, he did. With the whole cowboy getup he didn't even look handsome or young or tan, not even like someone who could be worthy of our mother.

Ashley stopped the car, and he waved and walked toward us, but neither of us made the first move to get out. "It's just one lesson," Ashley finally said, and unhooked her seat belt.

I sighed, did the same, and got out of the car.

Kevin had already picked out horses for us. "Don't worry, girls," he said. "These are my old grannies. Very calm for beginners."

My horse's name was Daffodil, which didn't suit

her at all because she was a dark brown color and sort of moody-looking. She looked about as annoyed by the whole situation as I felt. Ashley's horse was named Prancer. Prancer had a jet-black coat and looked a little saggy under the burden of age and work, but you could tell that she must've been really beautiful once.

Kevin said that for today, we were just going to get acquainted with the horses, and then next time we could really start to learn to ride. Ashley and I exchanged looks, but neither of us had the guts to tell him this was a one-shot deal.

Ashley went first, and Kevin helped her get up on the saddle. I watched him lead the two of them around the ring. Ashley looked pretty on the horse, as if she were made to do something like this, like one of those refined English people who rode their horses in shows or something. Her ponytail bounced against her back, and her face shone in the sunlight, and just before she got off I thought I saw her smiling, which made me really annoyed with her. She was actually enjoying this.

"Okay," Kevin said. "Your turn, Melissa."

I petted Daffodil lightly on her back and she gave me a dirty look and grunted, sort of unhappily. "I don't know if I'm ready to sit on her yet," I said, thinking to myself,

If I could just get out of it for today, then I wouldn't ever have to do it.

"Don't be such a wuss," Ashley said, and I shot her a dirty look.

"It's okay." Kevin put his hand on my shoulder. I tried to shrug it away discreetly, by bending down and pretending to fix my shoe. "You can't rush it. Everyone moves at their own pace." Ashley stamped her foot in the dirt. Then she glared at me. "Well, that's enough for today then, okay? Next week we'll see if Melissa wants to give it a try."

He gave us each a little pat on the top of our heads, as if we were horses, and then he turned and walked back inside the house.

"Baby." Ashley gave me a little push.

"Bitch." I pushed back.

Ashley didn't say a word to me the whole way home, and when we pulled into the driveway she announced, "I need to take a shower. I smell like horse."

I nodded, but I wasn't going to fight her for the shower. I didn't notice a smell, and besides, I didn't have anywhere important to go anyway.

I saw Ryan was outside, walking away from his mailbox, so I got out of the car and waved. He started walking toward me. "Where's Courtney?" I asked.

"I dunno. She had to do something with her mom. Spa day or something."

I wondered if they were going to Belleza, where my mom was at work, and I hoped not. My mom had never met Courtney, but the thought of her styling Courtney's hair annoyed me for some reason. "Ashley and I were riding horses," I said, which sort of hid the truth of the matter, that I'd been too scared to actually ride.

"Seriously?"

"Yeah. My mom's boyfriend has a ranch." It was strange that I hadn't told him any of this, because we used to tell each other everything at the moment that it happened.

"The Hair?"

I thought for a minute. "Actually, we should call him the Cowboy."

He shook his head. "The Cowboy. Seriously." He paused. "So how was the riding?"

"Well." I tried to look like I was searching for the perfect words to sum up the experience. "It was kind of like riding a bike," I lied, "only higher up and a little bumpier."

"Yeah, I went riding once. When I was really little

and my parents were still together, we went on vacation to this ranch in Montana. And they put me on one of those real little horses. What are they called?"

"A pony?" I guessed, though the amount I knew about horses could seriously fit on my pinkie finger.

"Yeah, yeah. That's right, I guess." He got this weird smile on his face, like he was remembering what it was like for his whole family to be together, and it was something he hadn't thought about in a long time, but now that he did it made him really happy. A good memory of his mother, not like the later stuff, the stuff that usually haunted him in the middle of the night.

I thought about the fact that Courtney had cheated on him in San Diego and that he had no idea, and a part of me wanted to tell him, but the other part of me didn't want to burst his little bubble. Before I could decide, he interrupted me. "Hey, you know, we haven't ridden in the wash in ages."

I nodded. "I know. You wanna go now?"

"Let me put this stuff in the house and I'll get my bike," he said.

It was a perfect February afternoon in the desert. The air was dry and crisp and just a little cool, but the sun was warm and beat down on us from the rich, deep blue sky. I took my sweater off when we got to the wash, and the sun felt amazing against my bare arms. I thought about the fact that Aunt Julie was back in Pennsylvania. She'd sent me an email last week telling me that they'd gotten six inches of snow and ice, and she'd had to shovel her car out of a parking spot on campus. At the end of the email she'd written, "Younger sisters rule, and don't you forget it!" which had made me laugh because it was so the opposite of true, at least in our case. Now I wondered, feeling the warm air on my skin, why anyone would leave this place for cold and snow and ice and digging their car out with a shovel.

Ryan and I kept a steady pace as we rode. We kept riding until our development ended on one side of the wash and Courtney's ended on the other, and we were just surrounded by that bare patch of desert on either side before we hit the railroad tracks.

Then Ryan stopped pedaling, and I skidded to a stop behind him. "You okay?" I asked, worried for a second that he'd forgotten his inhaler.

"I'm fine," he said. "I just wanted to stop for a minute and look around." He laid his bike down and started walking toward the side of the wash where we normally found the most interesting junk.

I put my hand in my pocket and felt the smooth piece of glass. I'd put it in there that morning for luck, or maybe just because a small part of me felt I needed to take something that was partly my dad's with me to spend time with Kevin. "Do you remember that glass you found the night my father died?" I asked him. I took it out of my pocket and held it to the light, so all the little rainbows started breaking and bending in the rays of the sun.

"I can't believe you still have that," he said.

"I never told you, but I showed it to my dad when I got home that night. And then he told me that it takes glass a million years to decay. And that was it. The last thing he ever said to me." I bit my tongue to try to hold back tears. It wasn't like me to get so emotional, but the morning with Kevin had set something going in my mind, the fear that I would have to spend the rest of my life going back home to a place that smelled like horses, with a man who wasn't and never could be anything like my father.

"That's really cool," Ryan said. "A million years." He didn't say anything for a minute. Then he said, "You know the last thing my mother ever said to me was 'Clean your room.' I was seven." He paused. "Of course, it's not the same thing. She's still alive. I guess."

I never thought about the fact that Ryan's mother was alive and out there somewhere. I'd never met her, and in all our years of being friends, he'd barely even talked about her. "Do you ever think about trying to find her?" I asked.

He shook his head. "No. No way." He paused. "I mean she should want to find me, right?"

"Maybe she does."

"What about you?" He asked. "Did you figure out another way to find that woman you were looking for?" I shook my head. I thought about reminding him that he had offered to help, but we were standing close now and looking each other straight in the eyes, which, for some reason, made me want to stop talking.

I never really noticed Ryan's eyes before, how nice they were. They were this deep blue color that made me think of Lake Mead, bright and sparkling in the sun. He was looking at my eyes too. His face was close enough to mine that I could feel his breathing, not raspy and asthmatic now, but quiet and even. I had this strange feeling that he was about to kiss me.

Then it was as if he remembered where he was and who he was with, because he shook his head a little bit as if waking up from a strange dream, and he took a step back. I stuffed the piece of glass back in my pocket and shuffled my feet, not wanting to look directly at him, not wanting to see it in his face that he was embarrassed or ashamed or annoyed.

"I need to get back," he said, and hopped on his bike. "I'm supposed to meet Courtney at four."

I looked at my watch. It was 3:55. He was going to be late. He'd forgotten about her for a while, a thought that left me feeling strangely satisfied.

chapter *15*

Courtney and Ryan decided to name their pig Miss Piggy, even though they were already pretty sure it was a boy. "We have to stick with the whole theme," Ryan said, and I could tell Courtney couldn't care less what the pig was called as long as she didn't have to touch the thing. Jeffrey asked me if I wanted to name our pig, and I lied and said no, because I really didn't want to do anything with him. But in my head, I secretly named it Wilbur, like the pig in *Charlotte's Web*, because I thought his face looked all sad, like he'd known he was going to die and there was nothing he could've done to stop it.

At least Jeffrey didn't mind doing all the work, and he

didn't even complain when I just copied all his answers from his worksheets without even asking, so I guess it could've been much worse.

I emailed Aunt Julie all about the pig. At first, when I sat down to write to her, I thought about asking her about Sally Bedford. She knew so much about my mother's past—maybe she would know about this too. But after I wrote it all down, I felt weird having it in writing, proof of my inability to stop obsessing over my father's life. So I wrote about dissecting the pig instead, as if it were the strangest and most interesting thing I had to report in my life at the moment. In response she wrote, "VEGAN IS A WAY OF LIFE," in all caps, like she was shouting it at me across three thousand miles. I wasn't exactly sure what a vegan was and how it was different from a vegetarian, so I asked my mom.

"Aunt Julie doesn't eat any animal products," she said. "No cheese or eggs or anything that comes from an animal."

I made a face. I could not picture my life without cheese, when I'd literally subsisted half the year on Cheez Whiz. And I thought it was a little weird that she emailed that to me. It's not like I was planning on eating Wilbur or anything. In fact, since we'd started the dissection, I'd kind of sworn off pork altogether, so in a way, I could see where Aunt Julie was coming from.

Ashley said she thought being a vegan was cool, and she was going to try it.

"Oh, sweetie, no," my mom said. "You have to eat more than rabbit food. You're already so thin."

Ashley shook her head and sighed. "Look at my stomach."

There was nothing there. It was flat, like a wall, like the pavement, not even an extra little ounce of skin. But I knew what this was really about. Ashley had gotten the application for her most important pageant in the mail yesterday. If she won this one, she'd qualify for the state pageant. And Ashley had never done better than place second before. "You're not going to win that pageant if you look like you just got off the plane from Ethiopia," I said.

"What's that supposed to mean?" She had her hand on her hip, and she hung her head to the side and glared at me. I shrugged.

"Girls, no one is going to get malnourished in this house." My mother stamped her foot down. "No one is becoming a vegan on my watch."

Ashley shot me a dirty look, as if this were all my

fault. I smiled at her and said, "I could totally have a steak for dinner. Couldn't you, Mom?"

"Hmm. Well, I guess we could go out." She paused. "I could call Kevin. See if he wants to join us."

How had that happened? We'd gone from a normal conversation to having dinner with Kevin, all in the span of thirty seconds. "I have a lot of homework," I lied. I had nothing, except for some poetry I was supposed to read for English and wasn't planning on actually reading.

"So do I," Ashley said, which was definitely a lie because I knew for a fact that she did all of her homework during her social studies class last period, where all the teacher did was show boring movies with the lights on day in and day out.

"Well, maybe another night then. Maybe Saturday after your riding lessons."

Ashley and I exchanged glances. We'd told her it would only be one time, but maybe she hadn't been listening. It was funny with our mother, how sometimes she had a tendency of only hearing what she wanted to hear. It was like that when my father first got sick, when they gave him some ridiculous odds of five-year survival like 10 percent or something, and my mother said, Well, Tom, that means 10 percent of people live longer than that, as if the other 90 percent never even crossed her mind.

"Kevin told me how much fun you girls had, and it made me so happy." She squeezed both of us, one in each arm, pulling us close to her. "I can't even tell you how much this means to me. You girls are so great. Really, truly. I have the best children in the world."

So there were riding lessons, every Saturday afternoon.

Ashley and I drove up to Dusty Meadows at one o'clock and stayed for an hour. Ashley and Prancer were becoming the best of friends. It was always like Ashley to take a bad situation and make it good, kind of like my mother, because you would never know from the way she acted that she didn't want to be there, that she would run into the shower the second we got home complaining that the stench of horse had followed her.

No, my sister was learning to ride Prancer like velvet. Her riding became smooth and elegant and sleek and looked like something she'd been doing her whole life. At first Kevin walked beside her in a ring, and then eventually he stood on the other side of the fence and watched her and called out things to her that she came to understand.

With me and Daffodil it was a different story altogether. We made no attempts to try and like each other. I gave her a dirty look, and she flicked her tail in the air and sneered at me. After three weeks, Kevin finally pushed me to get on her, and I did, if only to shut him up.

When I sat on the top of the saddle, I was uncomfortable and I felt like I was up way too high to balance. "You need to trust her," Kevin said.

I shook my head. "I can't." I tried to maneuver myself down, and when he reached out his hand to help, I took it. It was harder than I thought it would be to get down from a horse, and back on the ground I felt wobbly, like I was going to throw up.

"That was a start," Kevin said.

Ashley rolled her eyes. "Seriously, Melissa." She looked to Kevin to back her up. But he didn't say anything at all.

Finally, he said, "Everybody moves at their own pace. All right, girls?"

chapter *16*

In the middle of March, Desert Crest High went into an uproar. The week before spring break, tickets for the spring formal went on sale, and people started pairing up and breaking up and getting dates and ditching dates. Everywhere I went, there seemed to be this constant buzz of who was going with whom and who wasn't going at all.

It was a no-brainer that Austin asked Ashley, and Ryan asked Courtney. I was a little bit surprised when I heard that Max Healy had asked the Nose, not because I really thought he might actually ask me, but because I thought what Ashley had said about him and the Nose having something together had been an outright lie.

I just assumed that I wouldn't be going, and I thought I was okay with it until Courtney asked me to go dress shopping with her. Courtney and I hadn't hung out alone since that day she'd told me about making out with Mark in San Diego, so I was a little surprised that she asked at all.

"I don't know," I told her. "I've been kind of busy."

"Come on, Meliss. I really need your help. My mom's going to give me her credit card, and she'll drop us at the mall, and we can get whatever dresses we want."

She asked me in the middle of biology when Ryan and Jeffrey were busy digging through the pig. It was hard to see her eyes through the safety goggles, so I couldn't tell how serious she was about wanting me to go. "Well, I don't think I'm even going to the stupid dance," I said.

Jeffrey put down the scalpel and pulled his goggles up over his head. "I'd like to take you to the dance, Melissa."

I was caught so off guard by his invitation that I didn't even know what to say at first. Courtney started laughing and I kicked her under the table. "It's all right," I finally said. "I don't really want to go."

"Well," he said, pulling the goggles back down, "if

you want to go, I'm available."

I felt a little bad because the truth was, I did want to go to the dance, only not with him, and then I felt bad for the way everyone treated him, for the way I'd ignored him, ceased to recognize that he was even a person with real feelings or whatever, so I added, "It's not you, Jeffrey. I just don't do dances, okay?"

He smiled at me, his big, thick nerdy smile, braces shooting out over chapped lips.

"But you'll still go with me to the mall, right, Meliss?"

I said I would, just to change the subject. Just to shut her up.

On Saturday, Courtney and her mom picked me up at nine, and I promised my mom that I would be back in time to go to Kevin's ranch with Ashley. I have to say, I felt a little grateful for the lessons, that they gave me a reason why I could spend only three hours at the mall with Courtney instead of the entire day.

It was the first time I'd ever met Courtney's mother, but I was not surprised that she looked exactly like Courtney, only a little bit older. Not even that much older really, and I wondered if she'd had some plastic surgery. Ashley said that's what everyone in California did.

Courtney's mother dropped us off at the mall and promised to be back at twelve to get me home in time. Since she was a realtor she was always showing houses, and today was no exception. I thought it was a little sad that she didn't want to come look for dresses with us. My mother always took Ashley to find dresses for the spring formal, and they invited me to come along, though I never had. This would be my first official dress-shopping experience.

Courtney started listing off what she was looking for as soon as we got into the mall. Strapless. Not black. Maybe navy or red or green. Empire waist. Above the knee. I found myself smiling and nodding but only half listening. I was sure she would look great in anything. And besides, I couldn't get myself all excited about it anyway.

She dragged me to Dillard's first, which is the most expensive store in the mall. My mother and Ashley hardly ever went there unless the store was having some kind of great sale (which it wasn't). And it surprised me that Courtney didn't even look at the price tags as she pulled dresses off the rack that she wanted to try on.

I played the role of clothes rack and enthusiastic

nodder as she piled dress after dress in my arms, and once I was probably holding about fifteen and felt like I was about to fall over, I finally said, "Can we go try these on?"

She looked at me and laughed. "Oh, Meliss, I'm sorry. I got so caught up, I didn't realize."

I offered to wait outside the dressing room, but Courtney insisted that I come in with her. So we went into the big handicapped-accessible room at the end, and I sat on the little chair in the corner.

I tried not to watch as she slipped out of her jeans and shirt, but I couldn't help but notice. She had on a lacy black bra with matching underwear, and she looked like someone who could model in a Victoria's Secret catalog or something. Tiny little waist, curvy hips, and perfect breasts. It was hard to believe that she was the same age as I was, that she'd already grown into her figure and wore it comfortably, while I was still waiting for mine to materialize. Maybe it never would. Maybe I was going to be skinny and hipless and boobless forever. My mother said that some women were just built that way, like sticks and boards. I sighed.

"What? Don't you like it?" She already had the first dress on, a red shiny strapless one that would've looked ridiculous on me but of course looked perfect on her.

"It's great," I said.

"Do you think?" She turned around. "I think it makes my butt look big."

There was absolutely nothing about it that made her butt look big. "Not at all," I said.

"Oh you're just being nice. Tell me the truth."

"I swear. It's beautiful."

She sighed. "Truth is beauty, and beauty is truth."

"What?"

"Keats." She laughed. "Come on. Be brutal."

In my head I thought, You're a slut, and you don't deserve Ryan. And it annoyed me that she also had to be smart, that she couldn't be beautiful and ditzy but had to be beautiful and quoting Keats at the same time. But what I said was, "I really do like it."

"Hmm." She stuck out her butt and turned around and tried to check it out in the mirror. "I can't decide. This can go in the 'maybe' pile."

The "maybe" pile turned out to be my lap, and as Courtney tried on dress after dress, the pile on my lap grew to seven. The problem was, Courtney looked good in everything. She must have one of those body types that designers had in mind, because everything fit her, but in every single one she found some little flaw: Her boobs looked too small or too big; her stomach stuck out funny; or her shoulders looked flat. I couldn't see any of it. To me she just looked absolutely stunning in each and every one. Disgusting.

Finally, I said, "You should just pick one. You look good in all of them."

"But Meliss, I want it to be perfect. This is going to be our special night. You know." She looked directly at me and smiled this little smile she had when she was about to do something that she knew might get her in trouble. It was the same look she gave me in biology just before she'd go to cheat on the test and copy Ryan's answers.

I did know exactly what she meant, and it made me feel sick, right in the pit of my stomach. Then I wanted to punch her. I wanted to yell her stupid truth-and-beauty line back in her face and tell her she was hideous and a liar. I wanted to stand up and throw all seven dresses on her and run, and run so fast that I could run all the way to Ryan's house and tell him who Courtney really was, because now it was entirely clear to me that I didn't really even like Courtney. She may have been all shiny and pretty, nail polish and glitter, but underneath, as my father might've put it, she was a bad egg.

But Courtney, as usual, was completely oblivious to all of it, and when I looked at her again she was smiling and in the first red dress. "I think I'll go with this one. You like it, right?"

I nodded sort of dumbly, afraid to say anything to her because this anger I felt for her was horrible and was welling up inside of me ready to explode, and I wanted to hold it in and use it to give me the courage to tell Ryan what I knew.

I got home around 12:30, and even though I knew we had to leave for Kevin's ranch, I told Ashley I was going to find Ryan.

"No way," she said. "I am not going to horse-shit hell alone." She tugged on the end of my ponytail. "You can go find your boyfriend when we get back."

"He is not my boyfriend," I sneered at her, and in my mind I had this picture of Courtney in her perfect red dress, hanging all over him.

By the time we got back from Kevin's, it was nearly dinnertime, but I hopped on my bike and rode straight over to Ryan's anyway. All afternoon I'd been building my resolve, trying to rehearse this conversation in my head where I would tell him about Courtney and Mark, and he would thank me, and call her right away and break things off. And then he might say, Well, I already have the tickets to the dance, Mel, so we could go if you want to. . . .

I'd sat next to Daffodil and petted her back while she grunted as Ashley rode Prancer around the arena. She was starting to look like a pro, and I was thinking that if the whole beauty-pageant thing didn't work out, she could probably enter horse shows or something, but I didn't dare say that to her.

I felt my heart beating quickly, the blood pumping fast and steady through my veins, as I rode to Ryan's. I was nervous and scared and excited and joyous all at the same time.

Ryan's father's car wasn't in the driveway, so I put my bike down by the porch and rang the doorbell. Once. Then twice.

And then he opened the door.

He stood there rubbing his eyes. His sandy blond hair was sticking up in the back and he had on jeans and a white T-shirt and no shoes. "Oh hey, Mel." He yawned. I pushed my way past him into the house. "Hey, what time is it?"

"I don't know." I hadn't expected small talk, normal

conversation, and I was itching to say what I had to say. I looked at my watch. "Four thirty."

"Oh, crap. I'm supposed to be at Courtney's at four thirty." He ran into the powder room and threw his head under the sink, then tried to comb his hair with his hands.

"I need to talk to you," I said.

"Can't it wait, Mel? I'm already late as it is."

"No." I grabbed his arm. "No. It can't wait."

He stopped what he was doing, and he looked at me. There was water dripping from his hair down his face, so it almost looked like he was crying, as if a cascade of tears kept flowing like a river down his cheeks. And with his hair wet he looked like that boy I knew in elementary school, the one who'd had an asthma attack in the middle of a fourth-grade math lesson and had fallen out of his chair to the floor, causing Mrs. Tracey to scream.

"You found that woman you were looking for?" he asked.

"What? No." I shook my head. *No thanks to you,* I added silently. But suddenly I wished that's what it was, all I had to say to him, because oddly it seemed like that would've been less scary than this. I wondered briefly about what my grandmother thought Sally had done to my father, and if it was worse than what Courtney had done to him. "Sit down," I said. He listened and sat on top of the toilet lid, while I went and leaned against the sink.

"Courtney cheated on you." I blurted it out. I'd meant to ease into it, to try to soften it, but in the moment it erupted out of me, encased in this fear that if I didn't just say it I never would, that I wouldn't have the nerve to tell him. He didn't say anything, so I kept talking. "When she went to see her dad over Christmas in San Diego, she made out with her old boyfriend, Mark."

"I can't believe it," he said, and I felt this oddly smug sense of satisfaction. "Mel. I mean, I just don't believe it."

"I know," I said.

"No, I mean you. This is exactly what Courtney said would happen." The words rang in my ears, hard and heavy, like an annoying song that was being blared out of speakers way too loud, so at first I thought I'd misunderstood. "She said that you were jealous of us. That you were going to try to tear us apart. And I kept telling her she was wrong. But really, Mel, she's been so nice to you. How could you?"

I'd underestimated Courtney. Maybe she'd made out with Mark and maybe she hadn't, but maybe she'd set me up by telling me. Maybe she'd wanted me to tell Ryan because she was the one who was jealous, the one who couldn't stand the two of us being friends. "I don't know what to say," I said.

He stood up. "I think we're done," he said, running his fingers through his wet hair.

I knew he was right, that we were, but I wanted him to take it back, wanted him to reach out and give me a hug, or try to make me laugh, or ask me if I wanted to ride with him. But these things had all just disappeared in a matter of minutes, gone up in smoke heavy enough to transform the sky from something beautiful, brilliant, sunny, into something dark and dirty.

I let myself out. And when I got on my bike and started riding, I felt the tears rolling down my face, slow at first, then faster. I couldn't even wipe them away as I rode, so I just let them keep coming, blurring up my vision, as I pushed my bike faster and faster.

I was riding toward Grandma Harry, because I knew that even though she couldn't always remember everything, she was kind and loving and always happy to see me, and in some small way, that made me feel better about myself.

The thing was, the person I really wanted was my father. He was always great at giving advice or making me feel better for whatever reason. My mother had a way of brushing me off, whereas my father always listened completely and really seemed to take in what I was saying.

Right before he got sick, I auditioned to be in the fourth-grade play. It was some silly play about Sandra Day O'Connor and how she was the first woman on the Supreme Court, and I was sure I was going to get the role of her, the lead. I'd practiced the lines in front of my mirror for weeks, and my dad bought me this book about her life so I could study up and "get in character."

Well, it turns out, I didn't get the lead. I got the part of "Woman #4," which basically meant I had one line, and I was part of this crowd of people who watched Sandra walk by.

"Oh, sweetie," my mom had said. "Don't feel bad. Not everyone can be the star."

But my dad had taken me outside that night and lay down on the patch of grass in the backyard with me and said, "Look up at the sky with me, Melon."

I did, and there were stars everywhere, the way it always was, bright and clear and sparkling with constellations that I couldn't remember the names of. "So what?" I'd said.

"Point to your favorite star." I looked for a moment

and then pointed to the brightest and the biggest one I could find.

"You see my favorite?" he said. "It's that one, back there, the one that you can just barely see."

"Why?"

"The bright ones are just the closest ones, the ones we can see more easily. But that doesn't make them spectacular. That star I pointed to looks magnificent in a telescope, much better than the other ones."

"How do you know that?" I asked, skeptical.

"Because," he said, "I've seen it before, and it's absolutely stunning." He leaned over and kissed the top of my head. "Sometimes people just aren't willing to take the time to look beyond the things that are bright and big and shiny. You know what I mean, Melon?"

I didn't. Not really. But in a way, I did. I knew he was saying something about the play and how I wasn't all shiny and beautiful like Gwen Birch, who'd gotten the lead, or even Ashley, who had been thinking about entering a Junior Miss pageant that year. But that didn't mean that, underneath it all, I wasn't just as good as they were.

But my dad wasn't here now, and I couldn't even imagine what he might say to make me feel better about the fact that I'd just lost my best friend, that I was utterly and entirely friendless and that my social life consisted of Jeffrey's quiet and nerdy adoration of me and my Saturday afternoon dates with Daffodil. Utterly pathetic.

I stopped in the public restroom in the lobby and splashed some cold water on my face, so Grandma Harry wouldn't be able to tell I'd been crying. Then I walked toward her room.

I watched her from the hallway for a minute. She was eating what looked like chocolate pudding and staring at the TV. It sounded like the nightly news. I pulled my hair back into a ponytail and combed it with my fingers, and then I took a deep breath and walked in.

She looked up, a little startled, and held the pudding up, as if she were about to throw it at me. "It's you," she sneered. "What is it? What do you want? I thought I told you not to bother me anymore."

"Grandma it's me, Melissa," I said, fighting back fresh tears, because it was clear from her eyes that she didn't recognize me, that I was not her granddaughter but some other person, someone she didn't like. My mother had told us that this was a possibility, that sometimes her disease progressed in a way that would make her forget people, that when the memory ruptured, sometimes it started as a slow fissure, like when a tiny stone first hits a glass windshield. But then it kept on going, expanding, until it was a massive gaping crack, so bad that you couldn't even see the road to drive anymore.

She put down her pudding. But she said, "Well, I don't know any Melissa. You must have the wrong room then." She turned back to the TV.

I should've let it go, but I couldn't, because I thought if I pushed her to, she would remember, so I gave her what I thought was just a little mental nudge. "I'm Tom's daughter. Tom and Cynthia's daughter."

She narrowed her eyes a little bit, looked me up and down. "Liar," she spat at me. And then she picked up the pudding and threw it. I ducked and it missed and hit the wall. But the noise stunned me, like a firecracker had just exploded, right there, by my feet.

"I'm sorry," I said. "I'm sorry." I backed out of her room slowly, and then once I hit the hallway, I started running as fast as I could.

It was dark outside when I got back on my bike and started riding. I knew if my mom knew I was riding in the street in the dark, she'd be mad. She always made me promise I wouldn't, ever since the time a boy in Ashley's grade had been hit by a car and killed a few years back.

But I wasn't about to call her. She was probably out with Kevin anyway, and Ashley was out with Austin. So I rode my bike, slowly, in the bike lane, trying my best to watch out for cars. I wondered what it might feel like to get hit, if it would all be over too quickly for me to really know what had happened, or if the flight through the air off the bike would create a lull in my head, as if in slow motion, graceful and terrifying all at once, until I hit the ground with a thud.

I heard a honk, and it scared me enough to make me lose my balance and almost topple off, and then a truck pulled off to the side of the road. "Melissa McAllister, that you?" I recognized the voice, so I stopped and turned, and there, hanging his head out the window of a red pickup was Max Healy. "Need a ride?" he asked.

I was about to say no because Max made me nervous under normal circumstances, and right now I was a wreck, in no mood for any sort of company. But before I could answer either way, Max was out of the truck and asking if he could pick up my bike to throw it in the back, and I had no choice but to let him.

I'd never driven with anyone else from school other than Ashley, but Max was a more careful driver. I noticed that he stopped slowly and seemed very observant and cautious at stop signs, not exactly what I would've expected from someone as popular as he was—someone who drove around in a big shiny truck.

"So what are you doing out all alone on your bike at night?" Max asked as soon as he started driving.

"It's a long story," I said.

"Yeah? I'm a good listener."

There was no way I was about to recount the embarrassing events of the afternoon to Max, so I just said, "I don't really want to talk about it, if that's all right."

"Sure," he said. "So where can I drop you?"

"My house, if that's okay."

I knew it was Saturday night and he was probably going out. "I'm sorry if I ruined your plans," I said. "I mean you're probably on your way to go out with the No—I mean, Lexie."

He laughed. "What do you call her?"

"The Nose," I said quietly.

He laughed again. "Why?"

I realized he probably didn't know about her nose job, that maybe I only knew because she was Ashley's best friend, but it didn't stop me from blurting it out anyway.

"Oh seriously? That's funny. I mean, her nose isn't even that nice or anything."

The truth was, it wasn't. It was kind of small and awkward-looking on her face, so I always thought that maybe the plastic surgeon had given her the wrong one, like it was the nose meant for a supermodel or something, but the rest of her face was only just sort of average-looking. "Don't tell her what I said though. Please." I knew Ashley would kill me if she knew about this or if she even knew that I called her the Nose in the first place.

"Your secret's safe with me." He said it all seriously like it was actually some big, real secret and then he laughed again. He cleared his throat. "So tell me then, Melissa, what's a beautiful girl like you doing all by herself on a Saturday night?"

I wasn't sure what to say. No one had ever called me beautiful before. I was always the sister of the beautiful girl or, back in junior high, the smart one or the funny one or the friend of the beautiful girl. And I wondered if he really meant it. I thought about what Courtney said, that all guys like Max wanted to do was get their hands up your shirt, and then I thought immediately that she must not know what she was talking about because a) she'd probably been trying to sabotage me anyway, and b) my size-A-cup boobs probably weren't exactly what Max would have in mind.

Max pulled up in front of my house and stopped the truck. I unhooked my seat belt. "Thanks for the ride," I said.

"Sure. Anytime. Let me help you with your bike." We both got out and he reached in and pulled the bike out with one hand, smooth and easy in a way that made him look entirely strong and heroic.

He put the bike in my driveway with the kickstand down, and then he came and stood right next to me. I put my hands in my jean pockets and shuffled my feet a little. "Thanks again," I said.

He leaned in and gave me a quick hug, but I wasn't expecting it so it sort of knocked me a little off balance for a second. When he let go, he hopped in the truck and sped away.

I stood there in my driveway for a few minutes, the feel of his hug still hanging on my body in a way that made me tingle.

Grandma Harry and Grandpa Jack

Harriet Robertson was sixteen when she stood in the driveway in the hot July Phoenix sun and got stung by a scorpion for the first time. She wasn't wearing any shoes, even though her mother yelled at her time and time again about the shoes. "There are creatures out there," she'd say. Harriet rolled her eyes. Having grown up on a farm in Tennessee, her mother always seemed a little afraid of the desert, the whispers of snakes and howls of coyotes, and the sharpness of the beating sun. Not Harriet. She was fearless.

Until that morning, when she got stung by a scorpion the size of a sewing needle. It wrapped itself around her toe and wouldn't let go even after it had stung her, and Harriet screamed out in pain. Her toe swelled immediately and then her entire foot swelled up like one giant loaf of bread that had just risen high and even in the oven.

Her father was at work at the clothing store, and her mother was soaking in the bathtub, so it was only Jack McAllister, the new paperboy, who heard her screaming. He was halfway around the block delivering the afternoon edition of the paper when he heard it.

He ran toward the scream, and he kept running even when the sweat poured down his brow and into his eyes. Then he saw her, hopping up and down on one foot in the driveway, cursing like the drunken Merchant Marines he sometimes saw in his father's bar. For some reason, this made him smile. He could tell, right away, that this girl, this woman, she was different.

He approached her. "Are you all right?"

"Does it look like I'm all right?" She shot him a look of disgust and then she winced in pain.

He noticed the scorpion, now dead on the side of the driveway. "Put some garlic on it," he said.

"What the hell?"

"I swear. It works. I think my mother has some in the kitchen. I'll be right back."

He ran two streets down to his own house, a house his family had moved into only recently after moving west from Chicago. He tore in through the kitchen, searched the cupboards for garlic, grabbed a clove and ran back toward her.

He was bright red and so wet from sweat that it looked like he'd jumped in a pool of water on the way back. He was panting as he handed her the garlic. Harriet was not impressed.

They went in the house together and he watched as her mother crushed the garlic clove and chastised Harriet for going without shoes. "And what would've happened to you, had this nice young man not come along?"

Harriet grimaced at Jack, and in that moment he knew he loved her.

Two years later, after many, many dates, and some needling from her mother, Harriet finally agreed that maybe she might love him too.

chapter *17*

My father was pretty fond of the thing Newton said that for every action there is an equal and opposite reaction. He had it scrawled in the front of his journal as one of his favorite quotes, and he used to tell it to Ashley and me all the time, every time we'd do something we weren't supposed to or fight too much, and he always, always reminded me of this when I did things without thinking about them first. "In other words, Melon," he'd say, "there are consequences for everything." I wondered if this had been true for him, if, for whatever had happened between him and Sally, there had been consequences.

I thought about this on Monday in biology, when Courtney, grinning from ear to ear, walked right up to Mr. Finkelstein and announced that she and Ryan were going to change lab tables. "Yeah okay," I heard him say, because really, I doubted he knew where any of us regularly sat, and I doubted that he cared. She turned and looked at me all smug and smiley, and I wanted to punch her in the face.

I tried to think of something really obnoxious to say, but the best I could come up with was that her butt actually did look fat in the red dress she bought, which of course, it actually didn't, so that didn't get me very far. And I kept my mouth shut.

When Ryan walked in, Courtney waved to him from the other side of the room and said, "Hey, Ry, we're over here now." He kept his eyes on her the whole time, not even looking in my direction once.

"Well, that's an interesting development." Jeffrey laughed. I glared at him. "I mean, everything okay?"

"It's complicated." I sighed because there was no way I was going to get into it with him.

Jeffrey shrugged. "It was only a matter of time, I guess. Everyone knows you're in love with him."

I glared at him again, and I had the urge to shake him,

to tell him to lose the nerd glasses and whiny voice and the chapped lips, and then maybe he could have a human conversation with me. "I am not in love with him," I said, but for some reason I thought about my aunt Julie and my uncle Frank, and I wondered what their story was. And then I added, "Aren't you supposed to be dissecting something?" I felt a little shaken by what Jeffrey said, but then I told myself to forget about it. What did Jeffrey know about love anyway?

In English we were reading Shakespearean love sonnets. I knew they were supposed to be all great, being that they were by Shakespeare and everything, but most of them just didn't really make much sense to me. He had such a roundabout way of saying things. I wished he could've just come out and said it.

Mrs. Connor was wearing a purple glimmery shawl and she'd wrapped her hair around her head in a braid. "Now who can tell me what Will meant when he said, 'Shall I compare thee to a summer's day? Thou art more lovely and more temperate'?"

We all sat there silently, and I thought about the fact that Will hadn't lived in the desert, where a summer's day was painfully hot, not something you would want to compare love to, or at least I didn't think you would.

I started thinking about Jeffrey's comment from earlier in the day, that I was in love with Ryan. Would I compare Ryan to a summer's day? Not exactly.

Then Mrs. Connor asked us to look at the end of the poem, the part where he wrote, "So long as men can breathe, or eyes can see, / So long lives this, and this gives life to thee." Maybe Mrs. Connor could see it in my eyes that I knew exactly what he meant, right away, because she called on me to give my interpretation. "He's saying that the poem will keep his love alive," I said. I felt the eyes of the class on me, staring at me, as if I'd betrayed them by understanding the poem so quickly, so I added, "Or something like that."

"Very nice, Miss McAllister." She waved the end of her shawl at me.

I thought about my dad's journal, the way his words, his writing, kept him alive for me.

After school, I noticed Ryan had chained his bike on the other set of racks on the other side of the steps, and I saw him and Courtney standing by the wall over there kissing. It was as if Courtney had eyes in the back of her head, because as soon as I looked in their direction, she turned around, shot me a quick—and dare I say, evil—smile, and then went back to kissing him. I rolled my eyes at no one, hopped on my bike, and rode it home.

I was surprised when Ashley came in a few minutes later. She slammed the front door behind her, and I heard her running down the hall to her room. I grabbed my jar of Cheez Whiz from the microwave and walked down the hallway after her while eating the cheese with my finger.

She had her door closed, so I knocked. She opened it and just stuck her head out. "What is it, Melissa? I'm not in the mood right now."

"You're home early." I stuck my finger in the jar and licked off more cheese.

"God, you're disgusting. Can't you eat like a human being?"

I ignored her. "How come you're not with Austin?"

She ignored me. "Hey, what's the deal with you and Ryan, anyway? Courtney told Lexie in PE that you were, like, all over him the other day or something."

"There's no deal," I said. "There's nothing." The thought of Courtney telling everyone that I was some kind of creep who couldn't keep my hands off her boyfriend really burned me. I thought about what kind of rumor I could spread about her. And my first thought popped out. "Courtney's boobs are totally fake," I lied.

"Really?" Ashley opened the door a little wider. "How do you know?"

"She told me. Her mom bought them for her as a present when they moved out here. To make her feel better about the divorce and all."

Ashley moved to sit on the bed, and I and the jar of Cheez Whiz followed her. "Interesting. No wonder why they always look so perfect." She stood up and looked at her profile in the mirror. "God, I need a boob job."

"No you don't." Ashley's boobs were average sized and normal-looking, and she could wear nice V-neck shirts and they looked fine, not like me. "If anyone does, I do."

She ignored me. "Do you think Mom will let me get one, if I win this pageant? With the money, I mean."

I shook my head. There was no way in hell my mother was letting Ashley get a boob job. She hadn't caved on the nose job, even though Ashley had argued for weeks about that one. "She'll probably make you put it away for college."

She sighed. "Well, it will be my money. I should be able to do what I want with it."

I supposed she had a point, but there was still no way it was going to happen.

Her phone rang, and she said, "Oh that's Lexie. Get out, okay? I need to talk to her."

I took my time getting up from the bed and walking out, so I heard Ashley say, "You will never guess who has fake boobs."

And that was the first thing all day that made me smile.

My aunt Julie called a few days later and announced that she and Uncle Frank were going to Greece for their college's spring break.

"Ooh, Greece," I heard my mother say. "Sounds romantic, Jules." That made me think that whatever problems my aunt and uncle were having, they were working them out. I knew it was wrong of me, but I was a little disappointed. In the back of my head I'd been thinking that if Aunt Julie and Uncle Frank got divorced, she might move back here permanently. And this was a prospect that excited me, even though I knew it was probably something that would make my aunt Julie miserable.

"So who are you going to this dance with?" Aunt

Julie asked when my mother handed the phone over to me.

"No one. I'm not going."

"What about your friend? What was his name?"

I didn't answer her. "Ashley's going," I said.

She sighed. "When I was your age, I was always too busy trying to be smart to go to dances. I didn't realize you could do both, you know, do well in school and have fun."

I didn't clarify that I wasn't too busy being smart as of late, and that my biology grade was barely teetering on the edge of a C, or that the reason that I wasn't going was because no one, save the nerdiest boy at school, had even asked. "So if you didn't go to dances," I said, "how did you and Uncle Frank end up together?"

"Oh." She laughed. "It was pretty simple, really. We knew each other in high school, and we both got into Penn. So there we were, three thousand miles away from home, not knowing anyone else." She sighed. "And we were both a little lonely at first."

I had expected some grand and romantic story, and this one was turning out to be a little pathetic. "When did you realize that you were madly in love?" I asked, hoping she would just skip to the good part.

She laughed. "Oh, honey, I don't know. I'm a little more practical than that. You know, sometimes you just get used to being with a person, and then it seems harder to stop than to just keep on being with them."

"Uh-huh," I said, like I knew exactly what she was talking about. But it didn't seem like that was really love.

My mother took a few days off from the salon over our spring break so she and Ashley could go shopping and get ready for the spring formal and the pageant, which was exactly a week after the formal.

"There is so much to do," my mother said, scribbling a list for herself on a paper napkin. She looked flushed and hurried and excited all at once, and I wished briefly that I could enter a pageant, that she could get that excited over something I was doing.

Ashley was in the bathroom giving herself an apricot facial, trying to bring out the glow in her skin, and I was thinking about the fact that I had absolutely nothing planned for the whole week, save trying to figure out another way to find Sally. But I was sort of at a loss. The best idea I'd had lately was to save my lunch money for the rest of the year and then try to hire a private detective in the summer. I knew it was a ridiculous notion, pathetic even, but it was all I had at the moment, other than to ask Aunt Julie the next time I talked to her.

"Can I come with you guys to the mall?" I asked my mom. She looked up, surprised, and I knew it was because I'd never wanted to go with them before. But I'd reached a new level of boredom and desperation. "Maybe you could drop me off at the bookstore," I said.

"Of course." She paused. "Don't you have any plans with Ryan?"

I shook my head and thought about whether I should tell her the truth or not. Finally, I said. "We're not really friends anymore."

"You're not? Well, when did this happen?"

I shrugged, and I felt close to tears. Before I could stop it, the whole story came pouring out of me, every terrible second, right down to the last part about me lying about Courtney getting a boob job.

I was waiting for her to brush me off and tell me it wasn't a big deal or that I'd get over it. But she didn't say anything. She reached out and pulled me into a hug and held me really tightly against her. "Melissa," she whispered into my hair. "Oh, sweetie." And then she said, "Boys are idiots."

"Not all of them," I whispered. "Not Dad."

She shook her head. "Your dad had his moments. That's for sure." The way she said it, completely naked and honest and quiet, made me wonder for the first time if Ryan had been right, if Sally Bedford had been someone my father had been having an affair with. But I quickly shook the thought out of my head. Not him. No way. I silently vowed that I would figure out some way to keep looking for her, to figure out exactly who she was, if only to prove Ryan wrong.

She stood up. "Ashley," she called. "Ashley, come in here for a sec."

Ashley walked in wearing an old shirt, her face covered in apricot junk, her hair piled messily on top of her head. It was interesting the way these supposed beauty rituals made you look incredibly ugly while you were doing them, and I had to suppress the urge to laugh at her. "What is it?" She sounded annoyed.

"You need to get your sister a date for this dance."

She looked like she'd just been hit in the stomach with a soccer ball or something, as if the wind had been knocked right out of her. I was about to protest, to say I didn't need a date, that I didn't even want to go. But I was enjoying Ashley's sense of shock too much, so I kept my mouth shut. "Well, what do you expect me to do?" she finally said. "It's not my fault if no one wants to go with her."

That last part was not entirely true, but there was no way I was telling them about Jeffrey's offer to take me.

"You have a lot of friends," my mother said. "You must know someone." Ashley shook her head. "Just try. For me."

"Okay. Whatever." Ashley shot me a dirty look, which looked especially evil, layered in globs of apricot. And we both knew that she wouldn't, that she was only saying it to appease my mother.

"And you, Miss Melissa, you are going dress shopping with us today."

"I am?"

"We are going to find you a fabulous dress for this dance. Both of you," she said. She put one arm around Ashley and the other arm around me, and squeezed us both to her. "Oh, I just love you girls so much," she said.

So I ended up back at the mall, dress shopping again.

I didn't have a list of qualifications. I didn't have a color in mind. I wanted something that looked good on me. In other words, something that gave me the appearance of having a real body.

Ashley needed two dresses. One for the spring formal and one for the pageant, and she currently required a size 00, which is apparently incredibly hard to find. My mom tried to convince her to try on some size 0s and 2s with the promise that she would take them in, which Ashley wasn't too happy about, but she finally caved once she saw how minimal her selection was otherwise.

I was trying on dresses in size 2, which Ashley looked at in disdain but that my mother said most other girls would kill to wear. But I didn't care all that much about sizes the way Ashley did.

I tried on about ten dresses that all made me look too flat chested and straight hipped, until I found this one I really liked. It was a dark shade of pink and it was knee length and flowy so it didn't emphasize my hips. And it had this really nice, straight neckline that didn't emphasize my lack of boobs. It had this cute little cap sleeve that even Ashley thought was nice. "Oh, that is definitely the one," my mother said. I twirled around, and I felt oddly and imminently beautiful, as if the dress had the ability to transform me into something or someone else. In it, I could be the pretty girl, the pageant queen.

"Yeah, now you just need a guy," Ashley muttered

under her breath so I heard her, but I didn't think my mom did because she didn't say anything.

I went back into the dressing room and took it off without looking at myself in the mirror again. I probably was never going to get to wear it anyway.

Ashley and my mother spent the rest of the week shopping, and Ashley ended up with two amazing size-0 dresses that my mother had to take in at the waist: a black short, shimmery one for the formal and a long dark green sequiny one for the pageant.

I put my dress in the back of my closet and promised myself that I wasn't going to take it out and try it on or even look at it.

chapter *18*

The week after spring break was pure chaos at our school as people buzzed about the formal. We got to vote for who the king and queen of the dance would be, and Ashley, Austin, and Max were all in the running. I would never tell Ashley, but I turned my ballot in having only voted for Max.

Some of the popular people coupled and uncoupled and then coupled again, making it kind of confusing who was going with whom, but Ashley and Austin and Max and the Nose all remained together, and I remained dateless.

My mother bugged Ashley about it nightly at dinner, to which Ashley kept replying, "I'm trying, all right?

These things take time." And then she'd kick my shin so hard under the table that I had bruises to show for it.

Until something very terrible, stunning, and—might I add—divinely miraculous happened the Thursday before the dance.

Ashley broke down in tears as she heard the news on the phone. I'd wandered into her bedroom and saw her crying, and my first thought was that Austin had broken up with her. "Get out," she whispered, and motioned at me with her hand, but I pretended not to notice and sat down on her bed and picked up a magazine.

A minute later she was off the phone and blowing her nose into a Kleenex. "Jeez, what is it?" I said, thinking this was an awful lot of crying over a boy. And then I thought, Well, at least I'm not going to be the only one sitting at home on the night of the formal.

"It's Lexie," Ashley sobbed.

"Lexie?"

Then in very un-Ashley-like fashion, she broke down and told me everything. Apparently, for the past week the Nose had not been feeling well. She had a sore throat and swollen glands and a fever, so her mother took her to the doctor. This afternoon the doctor called to tell her she had mono, and she was absolutely, under no circumstances to leave the house for one entire week.

"No formal," I whispered. But in my head, I was thinking that Max, Max Healy, with the shiny red pickup truck and soft voice and strong hands, was suddenly dateless.

"Don't even think about it," Ashley said. "No. There's no way." She shook her head. "And don't you dare tell Mom."

Three hours later, as I sat at my desk trying to write an essay on the importance of rhyme scheme, Ashley barged into my room. "Okay," she said. "Don't ask me why. But Max wants you to go with him."

"You asked Max to take me?" I was completely stunned. I'd never thought that Ashley would actually do what my mother had asked and find me a real, genuine, amazing date.

She shook her head. "He called and asked if you already had a date. And I told him you would go." She paused. "So don't act like an idiot. And don't embarrass me. And don't screw this up."

Right then it occurred to me for the first time that the Nose was sick, and that she and Max had been dating, and I didn't know all that much about mono, but I knew it was pretty serious. "I don't know," I said.

"Don't be a jerk. You already have the stupid dress, and you know you want to go with him."

"Well, I don't want to catch mono," I said.

She laughed. "You're not going to be kissing him or anything. That's how you catch mono, stupid."

I nodded. "I know that," I said, even though I was a little skeptical that that was the only way you could catch it. And I felt a little annoyed that she thought I definitely wouldn't be kissing him, even though I also knew she was probably right.

"I'm going to go tell Mom." She shook her head. "It's going to make her day."

She left and I took a deep breath. I was going with Max. I was going with Max.

I imagined how I would look, walking into the dance on his arm, in my gorgeous new pink dress, how Courtney would stare at me with her mouth open and Ryan would just look a little annoyed, and how I would ignore both of them because I'd be so involved with Max that I wouldn't even be able to take the time to smile or wave.

Not only did it make my mother's day, but my aunt Julie's too. Just back from Greece, she sounded as if she were positively glowing, ready to burst right through the phone. "I hear you have a gorgeous date." She giggled to me from three thousand miles away, sounding much more like my mother than her usual self. I was guessing that her trip with Uncle Frank had gone well, and it occurred to me the way a guy could change you, just like that. I wondered if that would ever happen to me. She stopped giggling, and she cleared her throat. "Now, you know about using protection, right?"

"Aunt Julie!" I yelled, much louder than I meant to, so my mother shot me a look from the other room. I lowered my voice. "It's just a dance. Not even really a date." It would've been funny if it hadn't also been so embarrassing, considering what Ashley had said to me earlier.

Aunt Julie laughed. "Well, it never hurts to ask." She paused. "Oh, I'm so happy for you, Melissa. I want pictures. Lots of pictures. Promise."

After we hung up I remembered that I'd been wanting to ask her about Sally, but I pushed the thought into the back of my mind. I was going to the dance. With Max Healy. And I promised myself that, for once, I was going to live in the moment and enjoy it.

The next morning, as I chained my bike to the rack, I heard Max calling out my name. "Hey, Melissa." I looked up and waved, and suddenly I felt self-conscious about how I looked. I tried to smooth my hair down a little bit at the top of my ponytail. "Hey, thanks for saying you'd go with me, at the last minute and all."

"Of course," I said, trying to sound nonchalant, like it was no big deal.

"We're going to have a great time." He winked, and he tugged on the bottom of my ponytail gently before he ran up the steps. "I'll pick you up at seven, all right?"

I nodded. And I couldn't find a way to wipe the smile off my face, even if I'd wanted to.

That day after school, the day before the dance, Ashley and I had to go to our weekly horse-riding lesson. Since we were going to be getting ready for the dance the next afternoon, we wouldn't be able to go at our normal time, so my mom decided she'd leave work early on Friday, go over there with us and watch, and then we could all go out to dinner afterward.

This made me a little nervous because I was pretty sure that Kevin hadn't told my mother that I'd barely even sat on top of Daffodil, and I knew she would be expecting something more of me, a trot around the ring or something. "Can't we just skip this week?" I asked.

"Yeah." Ashley sighed. "I'm not going out to dinner smelling like horse."

"Seriously. What is wrong with you girls? Kevin is really excited to show you off. So I don't want to hear another word of complaining."

The three of us rode up to Dusty Meadows a little before four o'clock. We'd still have almost another two hours until it got dark, and I felt my heart drumming in my chest, my stomach churning. I didn't want to have to ride. It wasn't fair. What if the horse threw me? It would be just my luck to die on the night before my date with Max. Just the kind of thing this twisted universe would have in store for me.

When we got out of the car, Kevin gave my mom a big hug and a short kiss on the lips, like the kind of kiss I'd seen her share with my dad probably a million times. And then I didn't care if he was nice, if he had a gentle voice. I hated him.

"Hey, girls." Kevin waved. We both waved back, and Ashley leaned over and whispered to me, "What a dick." I nodded, though we both knew it wasn't true. He wasn't.

Once we got closer to the horses, Ashley put on her smiley, perky pageant face, and I heard her calling out to my mom. "You have to meet Prancer. She is such a sweetheart." I rolled my eyes at no one.

Kevin hung back behind Ashley and my mother and waited for me to catch up. "You gonna try a little ride today, Melissa?"

"I don't know." I shrugged.

"Well, Daffodil and I had a little talk, and she promised to go easy on you."

"Uh yeah. Okay," I said. "Maybe." But in my mind, I was thinking, No way.

"We'll let Ashley go first, okay?"

I nodded.

Kevin walked Prancer into the ring and Ashley mounted her there. Then he and my mother stood back behind the fence and watched her ride. Kevin had his arm around my mother's waist and she leaned into him, putting her hip against his, her head on his shoulder, so I started to feel a little sick, and I tried not to watch.

I sat in my normal spot by Daffodil and petted her back a little bit. "Sorry, girl," I said. "I don't think it's happening with us today." I walked around to her front and tried to look her in the eye. Her eyes were yellow and teary and reminded me of the way Grandma Harry's eyes had looked after her cataract surgery. "You don't like this any more than I do. Do you, Daffy?"

She made a little snorting sound. I reached up my hand to let her sniff me, and she nipped at it a little as if she wanted to bite it off. "Oww," I said. "You stupid horse."

A horrifying sound cut through the air like a glass shattering on a floor, sudden and irreversible. It was this primal animal noise, like the howl of a wild and crazed coyote that we heard sometimes late at night in the dark, heated pit of summer. Only this noise was longer and higher, and then it was followed by a terrifying thud, the sound of something breaking, like a tree that had been cracked with an ax. Someone screaming: Ashley or my mother or both.

I turned around, and I saw Prancer running wildly around the ring. Alone. I didn't see Ashley at first, until I ran closer, toward the ring, and then I saw her there. A lifeless-looking heap in the middle of the ring, like a rag doll Prancer had tossed aside.

For a minute it seemed like everything stopped, like the world had been turned on mute and slow motion, because no one moved and the screaming stopped, and then Kevin was running into the ring and carrying Ashley out over his shoulder.

"Don't move her," my mother started screaming. "Don't move her."

"The horse," Kevin said, calm and steady and quieter. "I have to get her away from the horse."

And then, as if she'd finally gotten her voice back, Ashley started screaming. "My face. Oh my God. My face." I could see her for the first time and her face was covered in blood, and she was hideous-looking. I gasped and held my hands to my mouth.

"We have to get her to the hospital," Kevin said. "I'll drive."

"No." My mother shook her head. "I'll take her."

"Cynthia. You're shaking." He sounded stern and entirely in control. "I'm driving."

Kevin laid Ashley down in the backseat of the cab part of the pickup, and he helped my mother climb up front. "Keep her calm," he whispered to me as he opened the door to the back for me. "And try to keep her still."

I sat down next to her, but I tried not to look at her. *She's going to be fine.* I kept saying it in my head, over and over again. *She's going to be fine.*

"This is all my fault," my mother said. "I made them take these lessons. What have I done? What have I done?"

Kevin put his hand on my mother's leg and whispered something to her that I couldn't hear.

Ashley whimpered, not so much like a cry or scream but more like the noise a sick dog might make. It reminded me of this thing I'd seen on TV once, of this puppy that had gotten shot in the leg and couldn't figure out how to run away. "You'll be okay," I whispered. I reached out for her hand and held it, and she squeezed my hand so tightly that I thought it would break.

"If I die," she whispered, "you can have my room."

"You're not going to die." I tried to make it sound like I really, truly believed it. "And besides, I don't want your stupid room anyway."

At the hospital my mother and Ashley went back to see the doctor together while I waited with Kevin on cold blue chairs in the waiting room of the ER. We didn't say anything for a while, maybe an hour or so, and I wondered why it was taking so long, how serious it all was, and when my mother was going to come back out to tell me.

I wasn't exactly sure what had happened, how Ashley had fallen, but I guessed it was either one of two things: Maybe Ashley had done something stupid that she hadn't really known how to do in an attempt to show off for my mother. Or maybe Kevin had stopped watching as carefully as he should've been because he was paying attention to my mother instead. So in a way, my mother had been right; it had probably been her fault.

Kevin had this annoying habit of drumming his fingers on an end table right next to him, and the noise was driving me absolutely insane, so finally I said, "Do you mind?" It came out a little ruder than I meant it.

"I'm sorry," he said, and he stopped. I noticed he started twisting his hands together instead, so it was silent but just as annoying. A few minutes later he said, "Your mother's never going to forgive me. Is she?"

I shook my head. Kevin had broken her perfect Ashley, taken her beautiful daughter's face and smashed it. Right then it occurred to me that the dance was tomorrow and the pageant was next week, and I absolutely knew that Kevin was right, that there was no coming back from this for him. I almost felt a little bad for him. "Maybe if it had been me," I whispered.

He shook his head. "No way. Absolutely not." He sounded so convinced that I almost believed him.

◇

Here are some things I learned immediately when my mother and Ashley walked back into the ER waiting room: The face and head bleed a lot. A broken nose does not require an overnight hospital stay, nor does a badly sprained ankle. If your two front teeth get knocked out, they can be replaced with very realistic-looking fake ones, only not right away.

In other words, Ashley looked uglier than all hell, but she was going to be completely fine. Eventually.

Her nose was bandaged, her ankle wrapped in a splint. My mom held on to a pair of crutches that I assumed Ashley would need, but for now she was slowly hopping. She also had a huge welt on her forehead that would later become this massive yellow-and-purple bruise. One of her front top teeth was gone, and the other one had broken right in half, so she looked like some sort of homeless crack-addicted witch who'd gotten in a fight with a hockey player.

And, apparently, she had yet to see a mirror.

"Am I hideous?" she whispered to me. "I'm hideous, aren't I?" I thought she was crying, but it was hard to tell because her face was so red and bruised.

"Well . . ." I said, trying to think of how to put it.

"Oh shit," she said. "Why did this happen to me?

Why do bad things always happen to me?"

I had to bite my tongue because in my head, Ashley was the beholder of a perfect life, to whom bad things never happened. Perfect boyfriend, perfect, beautiful body. Perfect friends. Perfect. Perfect. Perfect. And then it hit me, and oddly, it was one of the first times it ever hit me this way, that my dad was her dad, our dad. That his getting sick, our months in Philadelphia, his death, all of that had happened to her, too. "It's okay, Ash," I said. "You're still beautiful."

"You're such a little liar," she said, but she leaned on me to support her as we walked out of the hospital.

chapter *19*

The next morning I woke up to the sound of Ashley screaming. My mother and I both ran out of our rooms. "What's wrong?" my mother asked. "Where does it hurt?"

But Ashley was standing in the hallway bathroom, looking at her face in the mirror.

"Oh, sweetie," my mom said. "It will heal. It will all heal."

"I can't go to the dance like this."

"I'm sure Austin will understand," my mother said.

"No." Ashley shook her head. "He won't." She sat down on top of the toilet. "He'll just find some other pretty girl and go with her."

My mother walked into the bathroom and put her arms around Ashley. "Sweetie, not if he really loves you he won't. If a little bit of bruising is going to scare him off, then he's not worth it anyway."

But I knew that Ashley was right, that Austin probably was going to dump her, because that's how it was at our school. I couldn't imagine Ashley hanging on to Austin's arm the way she looked right now.

It hadn't really occurred to me until then that Ashley wouldn't go to the dance, that she wouldn't technically even be able to dance with her busted ankle, and that she would stay home and nurse her broken face while I would be the one to put on my dress and get my hair done and go out. I felt terrible that I was just a little bit excited about this prospect. "Why don't you call Austin and let him know what happened?" my mother said.

"No way," Ashley said. "We are not telling anyone that I fell off a freakin' horse. Okay?"

My mother looked at me. I shrugged, and we both nodded. "Well, we're going to have to tell them something, sweetie."

"We'll say it was a car accident," Ashley said. "Yes, that's good. That's what we'll say." She wasn't thinking about the fact that her car was perfectly intact, while she looked completely battered and broken, but maybe no one else would either. Why would they have any reason to question her? "And I mean it, Melissa. You don't tell anyone, not even any of your little friends, okay?"

I nodded, but the truth was, I really didn't have any little friends to tell, and I certainly wasn't going to tell Max. Oh God. Max. Just the thought that I was going to the dance with him later caused butterflies to jump in my stomach, and I felt completely unprepared. Ashley's accident had shaken me because it showed me I was right about not wanting to get on Daffodil all those weeks. The world was an entirely dangerous and fragile place, where one minute you could be beautiful and the next you could literally be broken.

All night last night I'd dreamed of Ashley falling off the horse, the sounds it made, the awful howl and then the crack of her face against the ground. In my dream I kept hearing the sounds, but I couldn't see anything and I couldn't move. I really wanted to help her, but I just couldn't do it.

Ashley stood up from the toilet, glanced again in the mirror, and said, "Oh God. Oh shit." My mother stroked her hair and didn't even yell at her for cursing.

Ashley went into her room and closed the door to call Austin, so I didn't get to hear what she said, but she came back out a few minutes later, demanding ice cream.

"Ice cream?" My mother sounded surprised. Ashley hadn't eaten ice cream in probably two years. "I'm not sure we have any."

"Well," Ashley said, "can't you go out and get some? I'm starving and my mouth hurts."

My mom stuck her head in the fridge. "How about some yogurt?" she offered.

"No." Ashley shook her head. "Ice cream. And not the low-fat kind either, the real fattening, creamy kind, and chocolate. Yes, definitely chocolate."

My mother stood there with her hands on her hips, looking perplexed. After a few minutes she said, "Okay. If that's what you really want. I'll run to the store and pick some up. Are you sure you'll be all right here? Melissa, you'll help her out?"

I nodded. My mother picked up her keys and went into the garage still shaking her head.

I sat down at the kitchen table next to Ashley. "I can't believe you're going to eat something that might make you fat," I said. I, of course, ate ice cream all the time without thinking twice about it. That's why there'd been none in the freezer. I'd finished it a few days earlier and hadn't asked my mom to buy more yet.

"Yeah," Ashley said. "Well, I might as well. I don't think I'll need to fit into those dresses anytime soon."

"What did Austin say?"

"None of your business." She kicked me under the table with her good foot, as if it were a punishment for even asking, for even caring.

"Oww." I rubbed my shin.

"Who would ever believe it?" She sighed. "You're going to the dance with Max Healy, and I'm not even going at all."

I was about to offer to stay home with her, but then I changed my mind because I was afraid she might take me up on it, and I didn't actually want to stay home. I was looking forward to walking into the dance on Max's arm, to having every other girl at school stare at me, even Courtney, or especially Courtney. Because just once, I wanted to know what it felt like. So instead I said, "You could still go."

"Don't be an idiot, Melissa."

Just as I was about to ignore my mother's orders to take care of her and say something mean, the doorbell rang. I jumped up. "I'll get it."

There, standing on the front porch, was Mr. September, looking a little forlorn in a pair of workout pants and a shirt. His hair was uncombed and not gelled like it normally was. I wasn't sure if I should open the door, if Ashley would kill me if I let him in the house. But then he rang the bell again. And again.

"My God, Melissa. Just open the door already," Ashley cried from the kitchen. So I did.

"Hey," I said, and gave Austin a little wave.

He brushed past me into the house, as if he hadn't even seen me standing there. "Ash," he called out. "Ash, where are you?"

I heard something fall in the kitchen, and I wasn't sure if Ashley had dropped something by accident or if she'd thrown it when she heard his voice. I ran past him and yelled as loud as I could, "Ashley, Austin's here," just to try to give her a warning, but it wasn't enough. Austin was in the kitchen before Ashley could get out.

I didn't think he saw her, I mean, really saw her at first, because he ran and hugged her and kept saying, "Ash. Oh my God. Ash." And then he let her out of the hug and stood back. She had her head tilted a little to the side and she was staring at the ground, but I knew she was going to have to look up and meet his eyes eventually.

Finally, he touched her chin, and she turned and looked up slowly. Austin gasped, his horror all too present in the noise he made, in the way he contorted his face. He put his thumb on her cheek and touched her nose softly. "Does it hurt?" he asked quietly.

It wasn't what I'd expected from him. I'd expected him to run, to freak out, to break up with her on the spot, but it hit me, standing there, that I knew nothing about him, nothing at all, and that maybe he was a perfectly nice guy who actually was in love my sister, despite the fact that he was a jock with a big ego.

I think Ashley was shocked too, because it took her a minute to answer. "A little," she finally said. "They gave me some Percocet for the pain."

He nodded. "You're going to be okay though, right? I mean you scared the shit out of me when you called."

She nodded. "You'll go to the dance without me tonight, okay? Take someone else if you want." It wasn't like Ashley to be selfless, to think about anybody else at all, so I knew she didn't really mean it, that this was a test.

"No way. I'm not going anywhere without you." He kissed the top of her head.

"Oww," she said.

"Sorry."

"What if you win for king," she asked, "and you're not even there?"

"So what?" He pulled her into a hug again. "So the hell what?"

She stood there in his arms, not saying anything for a minute or two. Finally, she said, "Okay. Okay."

I was starting to feel like an intruder, and I felt a little bad, so I tiptoed quietly toward my bedroom. It was strange, thinking about Ashley in a real bona fide relationship, where this guy, this really gorgeous, seemingly sincere, possibly future minor-league baseball-player guy actually cared about her, maybe even loved her. And for the first time, I felt a little jealous, felt like that's what I wanted. I wondered what it would feel like to have someone love you so much that they wouldn't even care that you were broken, that you were instantly ugly and smashed.

I felt a little bad that I'd been so quick to judge Austin. By calling him Mr. September I hadn't even given him a chance to be someone real. So I decided right then and there that I would stop. That from now on, even in my head, I would only call him Austin.

◇

Austin spent most of the day hanging out on the couch with Ashley, eating ice cream. "Isn't that nice?" My mother shook her head, so I didn't feel like I was the only one who was surprised by Austin's reaction. "What a sweet boy."

After Ashley fell asleep, Austin stood up and tiptoed toward the front door. "I'll be back later to check on her, Mrs. McAllister," he said to my mother.

She pulled him into a quick impromptu hug and patted him on the back. "Thank you, Austin," she said. "Thank you." He looked a little confused and maybe even embarrassed, and he just sort of shrugged and went for the door. After he left, my mother turned to me and said, "Looks like your sister picked a good one after all." She shook her head again. "Who woulda thought, a baseball player?" She got this funny little smile on her face, like she'd just thought of a secret that I knew she wouldn't want to share with me, and I cleared my throat a little to remind her I was still standing there. "Go take a shower," she said. "I'm going to set everything up in my room so we don't disturb your sister."

"Set what up?"

"My stuff, to do your hair, for the dance." She paused.

"I don't care what happened. You're still going to this dance, Melissa. And you're going to be beautiful."

I took a long shower, and I tried to think of witty things that I could say to Max. I was sure he was going to ask me about Ashley's accident, so I tried to frame this story in my mind, the version Ashley wanted people to know. I realized I should probably ask her what she'd told Austin, so we could keep our story straight. How weird. The two of us in cahoots. Like we were actual friends or something.

I had this brief moment where I thought about Courtney's red dress and the way her eyes had looked, all lit up and kind of mean at the same time, as she told me that this was going to be her special night with Ryan. I started to feel a little sick to my stomach again.

When I got out of the shower, I had this urge to pick up the phone and call him, to tell him not to do it, that Courtney wasn't really worthy of him, no matter what she looked like. And I wanted to tell him about everything that had happened last night with the Cowboy and the horse throwing Ashley and the way her face was bleeding and bruised. He would've been the one person to whom I would've told the truth and trusted with it completely. It was hard not to have that anymore, and I missed him in this oddly similar way to the way I missed my father.

But I was going to the dance. With Max. And I needed to get beautiful. So I put on a pair of sweatpants and went into my mother's bedroom.

I couldn't remember another time when my mother had tried to make me beautiful, just the two of us. There were the times when she'd practiced on my hair under Ashley's watchful eye or when I'd lie on her bed and watch her do Ashley's hair and makeup for a pageant. But it had never been just us, my mom and me, with me being the sole object of her beautification skills.

Last year was the first year Ashley had gone to the spring formal. The year before, my father was still in a hospice bed in the living room, and Ashley had been a freshman, a size 6 and not yet in a beauty pageant. No one had asked her to the dance.

Last year she'd gone with some guy who was friends with the Nose's older brother, who was a senior at the time. I'd lain on the bed and watched my mother pull Ashley's hair up in a French twist and make her eyes look dramatic with the green eye pencil. My mother had turned to me and smiled. "Maybe next year you'll go to the dance."

"She's only going to be a freshman," Ashley said, rolling her eyes, as if just because she hadn't gone as a freshman, there was no way I would either. Because let's face it: Even before she'd become popular, Ashley had still been a heck of a lot more beautiful than I was.

"How do you think we should do it?" My mother picked up my hair in her hands, and I felt like she was talking more to herself than to me.

"I don't know," I said. "Whatever you think." This was my mother's area of expertise, and despite a few lousy haircuts a year back, I decided I should trust her now.

She clapped her hands together and did a little jump in the air. "Oh I know. We'll curl it and put it half up." She pulled half of my hair back, so I could kind of see what she was talking about.

"Okay," I said.

She set to work with the hair dryer and then the curling iron, and I watched in her mirror as I was transformed into this other person. Someone with bouncy curls.

When she was finished with my hair, she did my makeup. I felt her layering it on, foundation and powder and blush and eyeliner and eye shadow and lip liner and lipstick and lip gloss. I'd never felt so covered, so hidden, as I did in the makeup. I felt just a little uncomfortable, because the girl staring back at me in the mirror looked like someone I'd never seen before, someone I couldn't even recognize.

"Oh you look stunning." My mom stood back and admired her work. "Oh, Melissa honey, look at you."

There I was, looking like a pageant girl, looking like a girly girl, looking maybe even just a little bit beautiful.

After I got my dress on and my mother found me a pair of silver heels in Ashley's closet, I was ready to go. "Let me get some pictures," my mom said, "to send to Aunt Julie."

When she got the camera out, Ashley stumbled off the couch, took a look at me, and then did a double take. "Oh my God," she said. She stared at me so hard that I wasn't sure if she was about to punch me or hug me. But then she said, "You really are a McAllister girl, aren't you?"

"Doesn't she clean up nice?" My mother was just absolutely beaming. It seemed like her eyes were about to pop out of her head, and that was the funniest thing about all of this. I liked seeing my mother all excited over me like she normally was about Ashley. I didn't really even care that much what I looked like, but my mother's reaction was worth savoring. I knew it was something I'd put away and take out again, the look on her face as she looked at me, as if she saw me for the first time as something truly spectacular.

"I'm going to bed," Ashley said, and she started to limp down the hallway. Then she stopped and turned around. "Have fun," she said. "And remember every single thing that happens so you can tell me tomorrow."

I nodded. It might have been the nicest thing Ashley had ever said to me.

Max arrived promptly at seven with a beautiful wrist corsage of white and yellow roses. "Wow, you look amazing," he said as soon as I opened the door. He was staring pretty intensely, so I started to feel a little embarrassed.

"Thanks," I finally said. "You look pretty good yourself." And he did. He had on a dark suit with a gray tie, and the suit fit him really well and made him look even more handsome than usual. As soon as he stepped in, I noticed that he smelled really good too, cinnamony and foresty all at once.

I didn't even know that we were supposed to get a

flower for him to pin to his suit, but my mother had taken care of it, and she pulled his out of the fridge, one solitary white rose with a pin. It was as if there were some secret white-rose code that no one had told me about.

"I'll pin it for you," my mom said, and she did it quickly and efficiently, as if she'd done it hundreds of other times before.

"Thank you, Mrs. McAllister," Max said. I could tell by the way my mother smiled back at him that she thought he was adorable. It didn't seem to matter that this was a last-minute thing, that I was only the Nose's mono replacement. Because right here, right in this moment, it seemed that Max and I were this thing, this actual couple getting ready to go to a dance.

Walking up the steps to Desert Crest High School with my arm linked through Max's was different from any other time I'd ever walked up those steps before. I knew it was something I'd never forget, that I'd think about it every other time I'd walk up those steps for the next three years.

It was as if I could literally feel people's eyes on me, feel them watching our every move, and not in a bad way like they were making fun of me or something, but like I was Cinderella walking up the steps in a fairy tale with a prince. I wondered if that's how Ashley felt when she was in pageants, if that's why she liked them so much.

The gymnasium had been entirely transformed for the dance. I knew there had been some committee that Ashley and the Nose had volunteered on to try to make this dump of a room look beautiful, and somehow they'd pulled it off. The entire ceiling was covered in pink and white and purple balloons that looked like tiny clouds, and there were balloons hanging on the walls too, probably thousands of them. So, except for the faint smell of old sneaker, you could forget that this was the same place where you had mandatory PE class and played dodgeball with the idiots who really cared about winning those kinds of stupid games.

One of the first people I saw when we walked in was Mr. Finkelstein, standing by a table of soda cups. It surprised me that he was chaperoning, but I decided he must get paid extra for it or something, because he looked even less interested in the dance than he did in our biology class. He sort of caught my eye for a second and gave a little nod, but he had this funny look on his face, as if he were thinking, Now how did she get to look like that?

A slow song came on, and Max said, "Should we dance?"

I nodded, and he led me to the middle of the floor, right in the spot where everyone could see us. If I'd chosen, I'd have danced on the fringe, right at the edge, but with Max I could already tell it was all or nothing. And he liked to choose the all.

I'd never danced with a boy other than my father before, but this was entirely different. I let Max put his arms around me, and I leaned into him. His smell was intoxicating, something that made me want to lean in even closer, so I put my head against his chest.

"You know," he said, "Lexie and I aren't dating."

"Oh." I hadn't known that.

"I mean, I guess she likes me or something, which is why I asked her to the dance in the first place." He paused. "But I'm glad I'm here with you instead."

There was something surreal about all of it, his voice, his body, his smell. I couldn't believe that I was actually here, that this was me, dancing with Max Healy. The Max Healy. And that he was telling me, or at least I thought he was, that he liked me.

Just as it was finally about to sink in, when I was beginning to actually enjoy myself, I saw a glint of red out of the corner of my eye, saw the blond hair, heard the distinct, annoying laugh. Courtney.

She looked beautiful in the red dress we'd chosen, not even a hint of fat butt. Slim and slender and model perfect. Her normally straight hair was curly and looped on top of her head, and she was leaning on Ryan the way a certain kind of large and venomous snake envelopes and chokes its prey. She saw me, and she gave a little wave. So I waved back.

Ryan turned around to look at me, and I tried to catch his eye for a moment, but he was staring at me with this strange sense of awe on his face, as if he didn't even recognize me with pretty hair and layers of makeup. Courtney pulled his face toward hers and started kissing him passionately on the mouth, so I stopped looking and put my head against Max's chest again. It was a perfectly nice, muscular, great-smelling chest, but I still couldn't get the image of Ryan, of the way he'd looked at me, out of my head. I wondered what he smelled like, if he'd borrowed some of his dad's cologne for the dance or if it was just his normal and reassuring Ivory-soap-and-Pert-shampoo smell.

"You're a million miles away," Max said.

"No." I took my head off his chest and looked at him.

His eyes were deep and brown and a little crinkly in the corners, and they were kind and interesting. "No," I said again. "I'm here. I am definitely right here."

"You are."

The song ended, but we stayed there dancing for a minute longer, through the first part of a fast song. Max pulled back first and offered to get us some sodas. "Okay." I nodded.

He left, and I was still in the middle of the dance floor by myself, not quite sure what to do. I saw Ryan standing alone off on the other side of the gym, and I made a quick decision to walk over and say hi. I told myself that I had nothing to lose, that I was being the bigger person—and besides, I was at the dance with Max, and that gave me this new sort of confidence I'd never had before.

Ryan looked incredibly handsome in a blue suit. The only other time I'd ever seen him in a suit was at my dad's funeral, and the suit had been too big on him then, had made him look like this scrawny little boy all dressed up in a man's clothing. But this suit fit him, made him look smart and tall and strong.

"Hey." I nodded at him.

"Hey." He stuck his hands in his pockets, and he leaned back against a wall of balloons.

"Careful, you might pop something," I said. I thought about how stupid that sounded and I wanted to take it back, to say something smart and witty and insightful instead, but nothing else came to me.

"So Max Healy." He shook his head. "Not what I would've expected. But interesting."

"I'm just . . ." I started to tell the truth—that I was only the Nose's mono replacement—but then I didn't because I wanted him to think that Max had asked me first, that he wanted only me, entirely. So I said, "I'm just not what you expect anymore, I guess."

He shrugged. "Okay."

"Hey, Ashley broke her nose and smashed her face up pretty bad last night." I blurted it out because I was dying to tell someone the truth, dying for someone to notice that I was here, beautiful, and she wasn't.

"Shit," he said. "No way. What happened?"

"Car accident," I lied, because I wasn't sure how much I could trust him anymore, and if he told Courtney and she told the Nose in PE, Ashley would outright kill me, and then it wouldn't matter how great I looked or if Max liked me or not.

I looked at my feet, at the way they sparkled prettily in the silver shoes, and I clicked my heels together three times just like Dorothy did in *The Wizard of Oz*. Then I closed my eyes and wished I could go back to that day when Courtney asked me if it was okay with me if she dated Ryan, and I wished I'd just said no and that I'd gotten Ashley to set her up with someone else instead.

"There's your date," Ryan said. I turned around and saw Max walking toward us with two cups of soda in his hands.

What I did next, I did entirely without thinking through, just spoke from my heart without running it by my head first. "I just want you to know," I said, "that I was telling the truth. About Courtney, okay?"

"Melissa, don't—"

"I swear it," I said. "On my father's grave."

I turned around quickly before I could see his face, smiled at Max, and walked toward him.

Max and I danced a few more songs, and I watched as Ryan and Courtney walked out in the middle of one of them. I leaned against Max's chest and tried not to imagine Ryan kissing her, pulling at her pretty red dress until it came off, until he saw her entire Victoria's Secret body. I squeezed my eyes shut tight and tried to erase the mental image, but it was still there, hanging around in my brain like some scene from a horror movie that I couldn't get rid of, that just kept terrifying me over and over again.

We stopped dancing when our principal, Mr. Forrester, stood up by the microphone in the front to announce the winners for king and queen. In a way, it was kind of like Ashley's pageants, everyone all dressed up and made up and waiting to see who would win, who was the most beautiful, the most popular.

Max squeezed my shoulder, and I thought he sucked in his breath a little bit. It was almost sweet, the way this was so important to him, but I couldn't relate. I never understood why people wanted to win these things, like the beauty contests. I mean, who really cared if anybody voted for you or not? What was it all going to mean in twenty years anyway? It's not like being Queen of the Rodeo had ever gotten my mom anywhere.

And the winners were—drumroll, please!—Ashley McAllister and Austin White.

Everyone was quiet as they searched the crowd, and it hit me that it might have been the first time all night that Ashley's presence was missed. I tried to soak it up for her so I could tell her about it. All the looks on the girls' faces as they arched and stretched to see her, what she was wearing and what her hair looked like. And some of their eyes fell on me and looked a little confused. Who's that girl who kind of looks like Ashley? And I didn't know Ashley even had a sister, they were whispering.

I leaned over and whispered to Max, "Sorry you didn't win. I voted for you." But before he could answer, I heard people clapping, and I looked up.

There with a black suit, gelled hair, and a swagger was Austin, walking up through the crowd and waving. Mr. Forrester put a crown on his head, and he walked off the stage and grabbed a girl to dance with. Not the queen of the formal. Not my sister. Not even an Ashley look-alike. But a cheerleader I knew Ashley hated because, as she'd told my mother on more than one occasion, the girl was a total boyfriend snatcher and slut and she wanted Austin.

I hated him, all his sweet talk to Ashley, his promises that he wasn't going to go anywhere without her, the way he'd sucked my mother into to this big fake lie of the person he pretended to be. I knew Ashley could do much better.

When the song was over, Austin and the cheerleader brushed past me and Max on their way toward the door. Austin looked at me briefly, shooting me a warning look with his eyes as if to say, Don't you dare tell her. And even if you do, she will never believe you.

I was feeling a little down after I saw Austin, and I knew Max could tell that something was bothering me because he kept asking me if I was okay. But I didn't want to tell him the truth, because I knew he and Austin were friends, and I didn't know him well enough to know how much I could trust him.

It was silly that Austin didn't think he was going to get caught. Even if I didn't tell Ashley, someone else was bound to. I couldn't imagine that Austin could convince every single one of her friends not to say anything to her. But maybe he didn't even care. Maybe, despite all his promises, my sister meant absolutely nothing to him. And that's what got me the most. The way a person could act one way and be someone totally different on the inside.

"You ready to go?" Max asked a few minutes later. There was technically an hour of the dance left, but people had started trickling out pretty dramatically after Austin's dance. It surprised me that it seemed to be the cool thing to leave the dance early.

Max and I drove the short way to my house in silence.

Not an awkward silence but a calm, sort of a contemplative one. He turned the radio on, but he didn't turn it up too loud, so the music was soft and made the inside of his truck feel mellow.

When we got to my house, he got out of the truck and helped me down, and he walked me up to the front door. Before I could step on the porch, he reached down for my hand, and he turned and looked right at me. "Thanks for going with me. On such short notice."

"Of course," I said. I nodded kind of dumbly, and I started to feel a little nervous because his face was so close to mine that I could feel him breathing.

"I had a nice time," he whispered.

"Me too," I said. I knew it instinctively, that he was about to kiss me, though how exactly I knew I wasn't sure, because no one had ever kissed me before. But I just knew, and I wondered if it was this instinct that women are born with, whether they are beautiful like Ashley or just normal like me.

I was so busy thinking about it that I almost missed it. So it felt like I hadn't seen it coming at all, because suddenly his lips were on mine, and in my head I was thinking, Oh God. He's kissing me. He's actually kissing me. I was thinking so hard that I was hardly feeling. His lips were warm, and they pressed up against mine, and I pressed back, and I waited for fireworks, for tingling, for a numbness in my head or my heart. But then, just like that, it was over.

He pulled back, and he smiled. "You are absolutely beautiful, Melissa McAllister."

I smiled, and then I turned and ran inside the house.

My mother ran to the door as soon as I closed it, but I wished she hadn't because I needed a moment to figure it out. To decompress. Max Healy had just kissed me. He'd told me I was beautiful. And I wasn't sure how I felt about any of it.

"Sweetie," my mom said, and I could tell from her face, her voice, that something was wrong.

"What is it?" I said. "Is Ashley okay?" I pictured Austin and the cheerleader twirling around on the dance floor, but I didn't know how she could've found out about it already.

"Yes," she said. "She's sleeping."

"What's wrong then?"

"Nothing." She pulled me close to her in a hug. "Did you have a nice time?"

"I did," I said. "It was fun." And it had been fun. The dancing and twirling, the eyes watching me, the good-night kiss. It was all something like a fairy tale, all very Cinderella at the ball, every little girl's dream.

But for some reason I still felt this sinking, this heaviness in my heart. I didn't understand it, how I could be beautiful and have had a perfect night, and I didn't feel elated. I didn't feel like jumping in the air and shouting. I wanted to go into my room and get undressed and wash the makeup off my face, crawl under my covers, and go to sleep.

"That's nice, sweetie." Her voice and her eyes were sad, and I wondered if it had hit her about Kevin all at once, that things would never be the same with them.

"Are you sure you're okay?"

She nodded. "Kevin sent flowers," she said. "Roses. Beautiful, beautiful purple roses." I nodded, but I wasn't sure what to say. I didn't know if she was looking for advice or approval or what, so I kept my mouth shut. Finally, she said, "You look tired. Why don't you go to bed, and we'll talk in the morning, okay?"

I nodded and thought that maybe she was right, that maybe the dull, blank heaviness I felt, that we both were feeling, was just exhaustion.

I went into my room and took my dad's journal off my desk, and I flipped the pages until I found it, my absolute favorite love story, the one I'd modeled all my own after.

Mitch & Carolina

They met in June 1920, somewhere in a valley in east Tennessee. Carolina Caplain was a farmer's daughter, and Mitch Robertson was a doctor's son. Carolina was expected to marry and harvest corn. Mitch was expected to go to college, decide on a suitable profession, and marry a rich girl.

Mitch's father took him to the farm to buy some fresh cheese, and while his father inspected the different kinds and the prices, Mitch wandered off a little and met Carolina, who was milking a cow. Somehow, he didn't notice that she was covered in dirt and her hair was a mess, because all he noticed really were her eyes, deep green and piercing, and he couldn't stop looking into them.

One night the next week, they snuck out and met in a cornfield owned by Carolina's father, and they lay down in the towering stalks of corn and held hands and watched the stars go by.

They did this six weeks in a row, every Thursday.

And then, the next Thursday, they snuck out of the house again, got on a train, and ended up in Phoenix, which was as far as their money would take them.

They got married, and Mitch got a job working in a clothing store. Carolina got pregnant, and just before little baby Harriet arrived, they bought a small house on the edge of town.

In time, Harriet grew, and Mitch's boss retired and sold him the clothing store, and then by the time Harriet was in high school he owned three. He worked really hard, and he made a lot of money. But still, every night he came home, he looked into his wife's eyes and he fell in love with her all over again.

They were married for eighty-one years, until Mitch finally died first, at age one hundred. Carolina, who'd been an incredibly healthy if not spry ninety-nine-year-old, died in her sleep the next night. She just stopped breathing, for no apparent reason at all. (Well, other than the fact that she was absurdly old.) She died of a broken heart.

Now this, my father wrote of his grandparents, is love. This is 100 percent absolute love.

chapter *20*

The morning after the dance, the first thing I thought about was Max's kiss and then in the next second I thought about Ryan and Courtney and their so-called special night and I pulled the pillow over my head and groaned.

I heard the phone ring somewhere in the distance, but I drifted back off to sleep, until Ashley limped into my room, nearly tearing the door off its hinges, she opened it so hard.

I sat up, and seeing her was still a surprise. The bruises on her face were more purple today, and the swelling was even worse than it had been yesterday. "Hi," I said.

"What the hell?"

"Good morning to you, too." I flopped back down under the covers. She ripped them off quickly, trying to inflict pain, the way you might tear off a Band-Aid from a cut.

"Max called Lexie and told him you two are, like, a couple now or something."

I sat up. "A couple?" The thought that Max had actually said that made me incredibly excited and nervous and a little bit annoyed all at the same time. "We're not a couple," I said. She glared at me. I went back under the covers until she pinched the fleshy part of my thigh, hard, hard enough to leave a big red mark.

"Oww. Stop it." I rubbed my leg. "He kissed me, okay? Just one kiss. No big deal." Lie. Lie. Lie. It was a big deal. My first kiss. And this was Max Healy we were talking about, the guy every girl in school wanted to be kissing. But I wasn't about to admit any of this to her.

"You are so going to get mono," she said, and she had what I thought was a smirk on her face, though it was a little hard to tell with all the bruising. I knew she was only saying it because she knew it would get at me, because for once, maybe, she was even a little bit jealous of me.

But still I felt this little bit of fear creep up inside my stomach like some wild variation on butterflies. "Max told me he doesn't even like Lexie," I said, my only means of fighting back to try and attack the Nose.

"Don't be stupid, Melissa." She laughed. "Do you really think a guy has to like you to make out with you?" She held up her two forefingers in a cross, and said, "Well, stay away from me, all right? The last thing I need is your mono germs." Which made absolutely no sense, because I was sure she'd spent more time with the Nose than with me, anyway.

"Yeah, well, I'm not going to be kissing you," I retorted.

She folded her arms across her chest and spun on her good foot to leave.

I could've called after her and told her all about the dance, about her winning, or about Austin and the cheerleader. But I decided not to.

After I got out of bed and took a shower and got dressed, I decided that I needed some time and some space to clear my head. So I snuck out my window and hopped on my bike. I wasn't in the mood to tell my mother all about the dance or have Ashley sneer at me or see my mother's purple roses stewing in a vase on the kitchen counter—thus the old escape route.

As I started riding, I thought I felt a little scratchiness in my throat. I wondered what the incubation period for mono was. I decided I'd look it up online when I got back. But maybe it was the warmer spring air, or the mesquite pollen that made Ryan wheeze this time of year. Even in the morning, the air was already thick and heavy with it.

I rode for a while, just letting my feet pedal me where they wanted to go, letting my hair blow back behind me, whipping around in the wind. I didn't consciously decide to go ride in the wash, but that's where I ended up, riding down the long, low stretch of desert alone, riding fast and furious and hard, until I could barely breathe and I thought my lungs were going to explode out of my chest.

I rode all the way to the train tracks, and I stopped when I got there to watch the yellow-and-black Union Pacific railway train glide by. I thought about my great-grandparents, Mitch and Carolina, whom I'd supposedly met a few times as a baby but had no memory of.

I tried to imagine these young, beautiful people jumping on a train like this one and riding so far away from home that when they got off they couldn't even recognize the landscape, the entire world around them, as if they'd taken a trip from a lush Tennessee valley to the moon: dry desert canyons and tall brown peaks, and dry, dry air that was sometimes hot enough to stab you.

I wondered what it felt like, to be so in love that nothing else mattered, not the time or the place or anything else.

Then from behind me someone said, "Hey." I jumped and nearly toppled over on my bike. I turned and found myself staring right at Ryan. "Sorry," he said. "I didn't mean to scare you."

I stared at him for a moment, and I tried to decide whether his face looked tight and worried or whether he was just tired and a little red from riding so hard. "I guess we both had the same idea," I finally said.

The words I'd said to him the night before still resonated in my brain, and I realized how stupid they'd sounded, how stupid they were. I should've stayed out of it and never said anything to him at all about Courtney, because I missed everything about him: being his friend, riding our bikes, calling people by their silly nicknames, and laughing over stupid dissections. And most of all, I just missed him, Ryan, this person who'd been a part of my life for so long that I couldn't really even remember the before, the part where my father was healthy and I'd gone to birthday parties and gone swimming in Kelly Jamison's pool. But that was the thing about my tragic flaw, being impulsive, not thinking before you said things. Some things were impossible to take back.

We stood there and watched the train together until it passed, maybe five minutes or so. Without the roar of the train it was almost unbearably quiet.

Ryan kicked his foot in the dust, so it swirled up a little in our faces and made him cough. And just to break the silence I finally said, "Fun dance last night, huh?"

He nodded. "I guess your sister was pretty mad about not being there, since she won for queen and all."

I shrugged. "I guess. I don't know if she knows yet. I didn't tell her."

He laughed. "Serves her right. All those mornings she drove past us on the way to school and never stopped to give us a ride." He shook his head. "Sorry. That wasn't nice, right? I mean with her car accident and all."

"Oh yeah." I nodded too vigorously, trying to keep the part about the horse in my head, even though it was just dying to burst right out of me. In my mind I was thinking, So what did you and Courtney do when you left so early? Where did you go? What happened? But I didn't want to know. Not any of it. Not really.

"So you like this Max guy?"

I shrugged. "Of course. What's not to like?"

He didn't answer. He kicked his foot in the dust a little more, and then I guessed he uncovered something because he leaned down to pick it up. "Look at this." He held it up so I could see it. It was another piece of rainbow glass, just like the one he'd found the night my father died. It was in a different shape, more of an oval, but it had definitely come from the same piece, from the same maker.

I thought about the fact that my dad said that glass could live for a million years, and I knew, right then, that this other piece had been there that night too, two years ago, but we just hadn't uncovered it yet. "Here," he said. "You take it."

"No." I shook my head. "This one's yours. I keep mine for good luck. You should have one too."

He dusted it off a little more with his hands and put it in the pocket of his jeans. "How long did you say glass lives for?"

"A million years." For some reason I thought about the way relationships were a little like glass, oh so precarious and fragile and vulnerable to breaking with the slightest wrong move—a cancerous cell, a tumble from a horse, a dance with a cheerleader. But even after they shattered, in a way they stayed with you forever, made you a part of who you are and who you always would be.

"I can't believe it's been two years."

"Next month," I said.

He nodded. "I know. I remember. April twenty-sixth."

The fact that he remembered, just that one date, that one tiny detail, made me want to lean over and hug him and hold on to him for a while and not let go. Because no one else knew that about me, that this was the date my world actually ended or this new crazy world of mine began or however you wanted to look at it. I was more a glass-half-empty person myself.

"You ever figure out who that woman was?" he asked. I shook my head. "You still want to?"

I nodded. I'd put her in the back of my mind with the rest of the craziness swirling around in it, but I did still want to know who she was, know something real about my father. "I just don't know if I'll actually ever be able to find her," I said. And that was what I'd come to realize, that there was only so much you could do to find a person, and then maybe you just had to let it go.

"You'll find her," he said, sounding sure. "I know you will."

Ryan got on his bike and started pedaling, and I got on mine and we rode next to each other. We rode and rode in parallel lines, just the way we always used to, until we got to our development, and he stopped to walk his bike up the side.

Just as he was about to walk up the hill, he turned and looked at me. "I'm going to break up with Court-ney," he said.

"Oh?" But I felt like I was about to roll back down the hill because it wasn't what I'd been expecting at all. I wondered if it was because of what I'd said, but I didn't have the guts to ask.

"It's just not working out. Nothing against her. Deep down we're not the same, you know?"

And then I knew what had happened after the dance. Courtney had planned their special night with-out telling him, and he hadn't been ready for it. Sure, Ryan liked her, but serious relationships scared him. And who could blame him? If my mom had run off with the gardener, I might've been the same way. "You're going to break her heart, you know," I said, which was a strange thing for me to say, considering I'd been rooting for them to break up all along. But it was true. Despite what I thought about Courtney now, I knew that in her own way she really, really liked him.

"I know."

"She'll get over it."

"Gee thanks."

I shrugged. But we both knew it was the truth. Courtney was beautiful. Courtney was resourceful. She'd have a new boyfriend in no time.

When I got home, I lay down on my bed and thought about Ryan breaking Courtney's heart and then what Ryan had said about Sally, about how he thought I'd be able to find her. How could he be so sure, anyway? It was annoying, the way he'd dropped out of my life for a few months and then popped back in, thinking he could actually understand anything that was going on.

I heard a knock at the door, and my mother opened it without waiting for me to answer. "Here." She held out the phone. "Aunt Julie wants to talk to you." I nodded and took the phone without directly looking at her. She blew me a kiss and left without closing the door, so I stood up and closed it myself.

"So," Aunt Julie said, "tell me everything. How was it?"

"It was nice," I said, trying to muster up some fresh enthusiasm.

"Oh. I bet it was." She sighed, as if she were almost living vicariously through me, revisiting those high-school years, those dances she wished she'd gone to instead of studying.

"Can I ask you something?" I said.

"Of course. What is it?"

"And you won't say anything to my mom?"

She hesitated for a second before she agreed.

"It's about my father," I said. She was silent, so I kept going. "This woman he knew. Sally Bedford. My grandmother mentioned something about her, and I think she used to work with him at Charles and Large."

"Oh, Melissa," she said. "Sweetie, it's been nearly two years."

"I know. I know," I said. "But I want to know." I paused. "What he was really like, you know?"

"Well, I'll tell you this: I have no idea who Sally Bedford is. But there is no way your father ever cheated on your mother, if that's what you're asking. Absolutely no way."

"Okay," I said. "Thanks." But that didn't really make me feel better. How could you possibly know something like that from three thousand miles away?

chapter *21*

The next morning Ashley begged my mother to let her stay home from school. "Everything still hurts so much," she whined, but I think my mother knew the truth, that Ashley was afraid to go to school looking the way she did.

"You're going to have to go back sometime," my mother said.

"Tomorrow," Ashley said. "If I'm feeling better."

"Okay. Tomorrow," my mother agreed, though tomorrow would end up being nearly a week, until most of the swelling and bruising had faded and our dentist put in some temporary bunny teeth until the new ones could be put in permanently.

I walked outside to get my bike, and I saw Max leaning against his truck, which was parked in the street in front of our house. "Need a ride?" he asked.

"Sure." I smiled. He opened the door and helped me up. He went around to the driver's side and got in. Just as he turned the key in the ignition, I noticed something out of the corner of my eye in the side mirror: Ryan riding his bike toward my house.

For the first time in months he'd come to ride to school with me. I thought briefly about asking Max to wait for him, to offer him a ride. It's not that I owed it to him or anything, after all the times he'd ditched me, but I felt a little bad making him bike up the hill, when I knew how awful his allergies were this time of year.

But I kept my mouth shut and let Max drive away. Once Max sped up, Ryan got smaller and smaller in the mirror, until he was nothing more than a tiny dot.

"You're not mad, are you?" Max asked.

I realized I'd been watching Ryan and hadn't said anything. "Oh no," I said. "Just tired. Monday morning and all."

"Good. Because I didn't know if you'd be mad that I'd told Lexie that we were together." He paused. "I mean I only said it because she was bugging me about coming over to visit her and about the dance, and I just wanted to shut her up for once, you know?"

I didn't say anything for a minute. "Are we?" I asked. "Together?" It sounded stupider out in the open than it had in my head.

He stopped at the stop sign, took his eyes off the road, and smiled at me. "Do you want to be?"

"Maybe," I said, and after I said it I realized I should've said yes, yes, yes. But "maybe" was the truth, was what I was really feeling.

"I'll take that," he said. "How about a date then, on Friday night?" He pulled into the parking lot of the school and turned off the engine.

I nodded. "Okay," I said. I thought about how Ashley was going to freak out when she heard about this, which made me smile a little bit.

He was already out of the truck before I thought about the fact that he hadn't said whether or not *he* wanted us to be a couple, but for some reason it felt like he'd already decided.

Max and I walked up the steps together and then parted ways in the front hallway after he offered to give me a ride home from school. He went off toward Austin and some of the other guys on the baseball team that I didn't really know but had heard Ashley talk about.

It was the Nose's first day back, and she looked a little lonely wandering to her locker without Ashley stuck to her side. She also still looked sick, and she had these deep, black circles under her eyes. Once I saw her, my own throat started to hurt a little bit again.

She turned and caught my eye for a second and glared at me with this look of pure and intense hatred, not like the glares that Ashley gave me but the kind of glare that came from a person who was secretly making a voodoo doll of you and wanting to burn you on a stake. I smiled back.

I walked toward my locker, and I should've been walking on air, but I felt a little down. I thought about Ryan pedaling all alone and it made me sad. Maybe I could ask Max to give both of us a ride home, and I knew that he absolutely would, but I also knew that I wasn't really going to ask him, that putting them in the same place at the same time would make things weird for all of us.

As soon as he walked into the biology lab, Ryan went and grabbed his pig and carried her over to my and Jeffrey's table. Jeffrey rolled his eyes. "What? Trouble in paradise?"

"Shh," I said. "Be quiet."

Courtney walked in a minute later, took one look at us, looked away quickly, and then walked over to Jack and Joe Beiderman's table—identical twins who were sort of quiet and a little bit on the geeky side. They obviously were not going to mind if Courtney copied off of them if it meant she was also going to stand there with them for an hour a day.

"You can't just ditch her," I whispered to Ryan.

He shot me a look. "Don't make a big deal out of it, okay?"

If Mr. Finkelstein had been paying attention, he might've noticed that there were now two tables of three and one empty table, but as usual, he wasn't. Or even if he was, he didn't care enough to say anything.

We were less than two months away from the end of the year and almost done with these poor pigs at this point. I was hoping I would pass second semester because I'd barely paid a bit of attention to pig parts, and I'd been letting Jeffrey stand there every day with his scalpel and this weird grin on his face. It had crossed my mind that if I didn't pass, I'd have to take biology again next year, nine more months of smelling embalming fluids and wearing latex gloves and tight goggles, and I told myself that I would study like a crazy woman for the final exam and hope for the best.

But I still couldn't bring myself to do more than watch, and by watch I mean that I stared at Jeffrey's hands as they moved inside our pig and let my mind wander to some other place. I felt a little annoyed with Ryan because, really, he had lousy timing. Why did he need to pick now to stop ignoring me, just when Max seemed to actually like me? It didn't seem fair that when I'd needed him as a friend he hadn't been there, and now I had to feel bad for leaving him behind.

"Hey," Ryan whispered to me across the table of pigs. I took my eyes off of Jeffrey's hands and looked at him. It was hard to tell what he was thinking with his eyes behind those thick, blurry goggles. "Wanna hang out after school?"

I didn't answer because I wasn't sure what to do. I knew Max was going to drive me home, and then what if he wanted to hang out? There would be no way to turn Max down, and I probably wouldn't even want to. So finally, I said, "I don't know. I'll call you when I get home."

I thought he'd be annoyed at my answer, but I don't think he was, because he kept talking. "I asked my dad about how we could find her, whatever her name was, the woman you're looking for."

"Sally," I said, but I was wondering how his dad would know what to do. He was only a Border Patrol agent, not FBI or anything. "Well, she's not an illegal immigrant," I said. At least, I didn't think she was.

"I know that." He sliced into the pig almost ferociously, and for some reason I thought about how sad it was that we were cutting this thing away, piece by piece, system by system, heart and lungs and liver and kidneys, until there would be nothing left. The carcass would be dead and completely empty and rotting, and it made me shudder. "My dad knows how to find people."

I bit my lip to keep from saying, Well, if that's true, how come he hasn't found your mother? But I also knew that maybe he didn't want to find her. And besides, it was a rotten thing to even think, and I was glad I'd been able to catch it before it had escaped my mouth unchecked.

My dad had known how to read people, how to make them open up to him and tell him stuff they'd never told anyone else. But that was a different thing entirely.

"There's this website," he said, still slicing into the

pig like it was nothing, like he didn't even notice he was doing it anymore.

"You should be a doctor," I said.

"What?" He looked up.

"You could be a surgeon or something."

He ignored me. "This site is free, and you can find people. Where they live and their numbers."

"She's unlisted," I said. "I already checked."

He shook his head. "My dad said everyone's on there. It's all from the public records. Driver's licenses and house deeds and stuff."

I didn't necessarily want his help anymore. But I wasn't sure I had another option at this point. "Why do you care so much anyway?" I sighed.

"Just let me help you, okay?" He put the scalpel down and pulled his goggles up, so I could see his eyes, round and blue and fierce and determined.

Max drove me home after school and parked in front of my house. He got out of the truck with me and we stood by the porch for a minute. I felt like he was going to kiss me again, and I felt embarrassed that it was broad daylight and all my neighbors might be watching, so before he could move in I said, "You wanna take a walk or something?"

"Okay." He shrugged.

I put my stuff in the house, and I didn't see Ashley, so I figured she was in her room. Part of me wanted her to know that Max was here and we were taking a walk together, so I tried to make a lot of noise in the kitchen as I threw my backpack down. But she still didn't come out, so I gave up and went back outside.

Max and I walked down the street, past Ryan's house, and I knew he wasn't home yet because his bike wasn't in its usual spot outside. Then we cut down the hill to the wash.

Once we got down there, we stood in the center for a minute, and we looked around, at all the houses off to both sides and this wide-open space in the middle. It had been a long time since I'd just stood in the middle here. Usually I was riding my bike as fast and as furiously as I could.

"You realize that we're standing in the middle of a river," I said. "That if we lived in some different place other than the desert there'd be water rushing through this."

He shrugged. "Well, when it rains a lot in the summer, it is like a river sometimes," he said.

"But doesn't it make you feel small, make you feel

like there's this whole big world and you're just one tiny person?"

"Well, no." He laughed. "Not really. It's just lots of dust and sagebrush and trash." He kicked an old beer can as if to emphasize his point.

I thought about the water, the power of the river, the way every other summer or so someone tried to swim in it and ended up drowning. What made me feel small was the knowledge that people could just disappear. In an instant. They could be here one night telling you some random fact about glass. And then the next morning they could be gone. Forever. But I just sort of nodded and murmured in agreement anyway.

Max reached down and grabbed my hand, and he started walking. We didn't say anything else for a while, which was okay with me.

It was nice to hold his hand at first, but then my hand started to feel sweaty and a little sticky, and I wanted to pull away. I didn't want to offend him though, so I kept holding on. Finally, Max stopped walking, and he let go of my hand. He turned and faced me, and he put his thumb on my cheek. "You're so interesting, Melissa. You're not like all the other girls."

I wasn't sure what to say, so I didn't say anything.

I thought about all the other times that I'd wished I could've been like Ashley or the Nose or Courtney just because it would've made my life infinitely easier to be beautiful and girly and popular. For the first time, standing right there with Max, I almost felt glad that I wasn't them.

He leaned in to kiss me, and his lips were soft and warm and nice, so I kissed him back.

When he stopped kissing me, he kept his face close, and I could see every inch of it. These beautiful brown eyes and this charming smile, and I felt a little starstruck.

I couldn't believe it. This guy actually liked me.

After dinner I sat at my desk, and tried to do my homework. But it was hard to concentrate. I was thinking about Max and the fact that he liked that I was different. So maybe I wasn't the most beautiful girl, but that was okay.

Ashley hobbled in without even knocking and went and flopped on my bed.

"Don't lean on my pillow," I said, pretending to be deep into my homework. "You might get mono germs."

She ignored me. "Did Austin go to the dance?" she asked.

I looked up. Her face still looked horrible, even though some of the swelling had gone down. I felt just a little guilty that I hadn't mentioned it to her before. "Yes," I whispered.

"Dammit." She flopped back against my pillow. I thought that maybe she was going to cry, but it was hard to tell with her face being so banged up.

"You can do better," I said.

She sat up. "What, like Max?" She laughed. "Don't be so stupid, Melissa. He's not really in love with you or anything."

I thought about the way he'd kissed me in the wash, and I was sure she was wrong. "You don't know everything," I said. "You're not always right."

"And you are?" She laughed again. "You don't know the first thing about a guy like him."

I shook my head. "What do you mean?"

She stood up from the bed and limped toward the door. "You're smart—you figure it out."

I was still sitting there trying to figure out what Ashley was talking about when I heard a tapping at the window. I remembered that I'd forgotten to call Ryan when I got home.

I stood up and opened the window, and he climbed in and lay down on my bed. I thought about warning him against mono germs, but then I didn't. I didn't want to tell him about kissing Max, and besides, I didn't think he could really get mono just from sitting in my bed.

"Get on your computer," he said. "I'll tell you this website, and we'll find her."

I stared at him, waiting for something, for an apology. I wanted him to say he was sorry for being a jerk, an idiot, a complete and total ass. *Mel, I should've listened to you. You were right. I'll never let a pretty girl come between us again.*

Finally, he said, "You can't stay mad at me forever."

I shrugged. Well, I could if I wanted to. But then I looked at him. His eyes were sort of lost and sad, and he looked really tired. And his breathing was heavy and ragged. Still, I didn't know if we could go back to the way things were before, if I could really, truly forgive and forget.

We were both quiet for a few minutes, and then he said, "Why don't we at least look her up, and find her number and where she lives?"

"Okay," I said, because I knew he wasn't going to leave until I did it, and even though I was still mad, I also still wanted to find Sally.

Ryan gave me the name of the site, and I typed her name in. All her information came up on the screen, a phone number and an address that wasn't too far from here. I was amazed at the way it was all there instantaneously, at my fingertips, but I tried not to let Ryan see how impressed I was.

"Let's call her," Ryan said. His voice was thick and asthmatic and excited.

I thought about the way he'd looked at me in his bathroom that day when I'd told him about Courtney, his hair dripping wet and his eyes dark and angry. I had the sudden urge to kick him the way Ashley always did to me, to tell him to drop the excitement, because he'd lost the right to have it. But all I said was, "It's late."

"Okay." He shrugged. "I get it. I'll go." He stared at me for a minute, as if he wanted to say something else but wasn't sure how to say it, and then he climbed out the window. I heard him drop to the ground, a quick crunchy thud in the rocks.

I picked up the phone and cradled it in my hand for a minute. I started to dial the number, then hung up. It was already after nine, I reasoned, my heart beating like a drum in my chest. One more day wouldn't hurt.

chapter *22*

The next day at school, I spent the majority of the day alternating between pondering what I might say to Sally Bedford on the phone and what Ashley had meant when she said that I didn't really know anything about Max.

I thought mostly of Max, except in biology when Ryan prodded me about Sally.

Ryan elbowed me with his left arm as he cut into the pig brain with his right. The ease with which he could now dissect amazed me just a little bit. "Well?" he asked. "What did she say?" He sounded like a little kid on Christmas morning, as if he was just about to burst, waiting to find out the details.

"I didn't call her," I said. "It was too late."

"It wasn't that late," he said. I glared at him, so he said, "Yeah, you were probably smart to wait."

"I'm going to call her later," I said.

He tilted his head to the side, and I could tell, even behind the goggles, that he was shooting me a quizzical look, as if he didn't quite believe me.

In English Mrs. Connor droned on and on about Keats. And I thought about how Courtney had quoted him in the dressing room. Could something really be beautiful and true at the same time? Was it possible that Max was good-looking and also the real thing?

"Miss McAllister?" Mrs. Conner said. "Miss McAllister."

"Uhh." I looked up, but I had no idea what she'd asked me or what poem she'd been discussing. I shrugged and she frowned at me. She had this way of looking oddly disappointed the way my father might have, as if she were telling me that she'd been expecting more of me.

When I went out to meet Max in the parking lot after school, I nearly ran straight into Courtney. She was rushing down the steps, like she was in an awful big hurry to get somewhere, and I was kind of going slowly, deep in thought, still thinking about the difference between truth and beauty and whether they were actually linked or two separate things. "Oh sorry," she said. She looked up, saw it was me, and smiled. "Oh hey, Meliss."

Just like that. No hard feelings. No mean looks.

She stared at me, and I felt like I had to say something, so I said, "Sorry about you and Ryan." Lie. Lie. Lie. But I smiled anyway. I was about to say that I'd just been thinking about her, but then I decided against it. I didn't feel like explaining.

She shrugged. "Yeah. It happens, I guess." She sounded all nonchalant, like she didn't even care that much, and like she didn't blame me, which surprised me in a way. "So you and Max, huh?"

I nodded. "Yeah, I guess so."

She laughed. "Well, don't knock yourself out with the excitement or anything."

"I am excited," I said, forcing a smile.

She sighed. "You don't have to pretend with me." She paused. "Everyone knows that you and Ryan want each other anyway."

I felt my face turning bright red. "No way. We're just friends." And right now we were barely that.

"Oh come on, Meliss. I'm not mad, okay? I saw the way he was looking at you at the dance. It's just the way it is. I get it." She leaned in and gave me a quick and forceful hug, which I didn't return. But she didn't seem to notice. "I've gotta run. Paco has obedience school in thirty minutes." She started running through the parking lot, but she stopped after a few steps and turned and yelled out behind her, "Call me."

I was positive that I was never going to call her again.

Max told me all about some baseball thing the whole way home, but I wasn't really listening. I kept thinking about what Courtney had said, that everyone thought that Ryan and I liked each other, and I wondered if that was true. I didn't think anyone else at our school would've even noticed us aside from her, and I knew deep down that she was just jealous. Still, there was something about what she said that made me feel a little uneasy and itchy all over. Or maybe it was just that I was starting to develop a mono rash that I'd read about online.

I turned my brain off for a minute and caught something Max was saying about some action movie he wanted to see on Friday night. "Oh yeah, sure. Whatever," I said, though I honestly hated action movies. I was more of a romantic-comedy girl myself.

Max shook his head. "You're so laid-back, Melissa. Most girls are so high-strung and prissy."

Laid-back was not the term I would've used to describe myself. Most of the time I felt tight and twisted in knots like a contortionist, worrying about all the terrible things that might happen to me and I wondered who this girl was that Max could see and no one else could.

When he got to my house, he leaned over and gave me a quick kiss on the lips. "I've gotta run," he said. "I'm meeting the guys."

I nodded, and I slid out of the car, feeling oddly free.

Ashley was lying on her bed talking on the phone, probably to the Nose because she was complaining about what a jerk Austin was and how he wasn't even a good kisser.

I flopped down on the bed next to her, and I put my head on her pillow. She kicked at my ankles with her good foot, but I didn't budge. I'd resigned myself to the fact that I wasn't leaving her room until she told me what she meant about Max. I couldn't waste another entire day of my life worrying about it, because if I did, I might not even be able to pass ninth grade. Then I'd have a heck of a lot more to worry about.

Finally, she sighed really loud, an exaggerated sigh

for the Nose's benefit. "I have to call you back," she said. "The freakin' imp will not leave me alone."

I hadn't heard her call me that in a while, but it still stung, every time.

She hung up the phone. "What do you want?"

"Tell me what you meant about Max," I said. "Or I'm telling everyone about the horse."

She gasped. "You wouldn't dare."

She was right, I probably wouldn't. I still felt really bad for her about her face and the dance and the pageant and everything. But I nodded. "I would."

She sat up and pulled her hair back into a ponytail, and I saw her face was looking a little better. The bruises were yellower than yesterday, and I figured, once she got her teeth fixed up, that eventually you wouldn't even be able to tell. "The senior guys on the team always go after the freshmen," she said. "They even keep a count of who can get the most freshmen to sleep with them before the end of the year. Austin isn't like that."

"So what?" I tried to brush her off. "Max isn't either."

"Isn't he?" She smirked a little, and I knew she took satisfaction in the fact that I was such an out-of-it little imp that I'd never even thought that Max might be using me. "Anyway," she said. "What other reason could he possibly have for ditching Lexie for you? You don't actually think he likes you, do you?"

"Shut up." I kicked her, hard, and I had to fight back tears that were welling up and stinging my eyes.

I got off her bed and ran into my room and slammed the door behind me.

There were no answers in my dad's journal, no stories that could make me feel better about this. His stories were about amazing people, people in love, things you would never believe or even dream. But they did not tell you what to do when your heart felt like it was being crushed, when your head felt like it was going to explode, when the most popular boy at school either sincerely liked you or just wanted to sleep with you so he could brag to his friends. They did not tell you what it meant for your best friend to look at you in a way that his girlfriend, well, ex-girlfriend, noticed.

I picked up the journal and threw it against the wall. "Useless," I muttered. Utterly and completely useless.

But then I wondered, even if my dad were here, if this would be the kind of stuff I would've asked him about, because it didn't seem like the kind of thing a girl could tell her father. Not that my father was just any father, so who knows, maybe he would've had all the answers.

I got into bed and lay there for a while, and I must've fallen asleep, because the next thing I knew my mom was knocking on my door and it was already dark outside. "Melissa," she called through the door. "Everything okay? Can I come in?"

"Yes," I said. "Come in." My voice was thick and my throat felt scratchy, and in the back of my head this little mono alarm went off.

She opened the door. "You didn't come out for dinner. I was worried." That was me. Always the eater. My dad used to joke that I would have to be dead to miss a meal. Ha ha. Hysterical now.

"I'm not that hungry," I said.

She came in and put her hand to my forehead. "You don't feel hot, sweetie."

"Just a bad day," I said.

She sat on the edge of my bed. "You want to talk about it?" I did. But I didn't. My mother and I didn't talk. When I told her things, she offered me generic words of consolation or told me to stop worrying, and I never ever felt better. "How are things with you and this Max guy?"

I shrugged. "I don't know," I said. "I think he likes me." But the little voice in my head said, *Or does he?*

"And what about you?" my mother asked. "Do you like him?"

"Everybody likes him," I said.

She nodded. "Sweetie, you should trust yourself more." There she was with her generic nonhelpful advice.

"I know," I said, but who knew what that meant anyway. "It's just, how do you know if you love someone?" I asked her.

She stood up and pulled her hair back into a ponytail with her hand the same way Ashley always did. She walked over to the window, and it seemed like she was looking for something outside. "You just know," she said. "You just feel it. Everywhere. All over."

"What does it feel like?"

"Well"—she thought for a minute—"with your father, it was like wind. Like this strong gust came and swirled me up around into the air until I was so dizzy that I couldn't even breathe."

"What about with Kevin?"

"Oh, sweetie." She sighed. "I don't know. I don't even know if I love that man."

I thought about the way she'd looked at the purple roses that he'd sent, the way she'd closed her eyes and held them up to her nose as if searching for a piece of him in there, and I knew that she did. I wanted to tell her that it was just an accident, that it wasn't his fault. But I couldn't bring myself to do it, to actually defend him, even if deep down I knew that he was a really nice guy and he, cowboy boots and all, genuinely cared about my mother.

I was also positive that, despite what she said, she really did love him, which felt like another reason to keep my mouth shut.

chapter *23*

Here's something I learned from my father's journal: When glass breaks, the cracks move at a speed greater than three thousand miles per hour. All you had to do was drop it on a hard floor, and it set off this reaction that came so quickly that you couldn't take it back, even if you wanted to.

I wondered how fast bones splinter, how long it took for Ashley's nose to break, for her teeth to crack in half. What I do know, is that from the moment it had happened, it took less than a week for the rest of her life to crumble, break, and shatter recklessly.

On Thursday afternoon my mother took Ashley to

get her transition bunny teeth put in at Dr. Langley's office. And Friday morning was her first day back at school. My mother didn't want her driving, even though it was her left ankle she'd sprained, because her face injuries were still so bad, and Ashley didn't want to take the car yet because she was lying and telling everyone it was still being fixed. So my mother asked if Max would give us both a ride.

"No way." I glared at Ashley.

"Melissa." My mother sounded sterner than usual. "If it weren't for Ashley, you wouldn't even be getting a ride from Max. She asked him to take you to the dance, remember?"

Ashley smirked, and I was backed into a corner. So Max ended up taking both of us.

For once I got to ride shotgun, and Ashley, who'd gotten in the truck with the help of Max, was in the back, which made me feel a little bit better. Still, I kept turning around and glaring at her the whole ride.

When we got to school, the three of us walked up the steps together. Well, Max and I walked and Ashley hopped, a sight that I found both hysterical and a little sad. Though she could get around without the crutches, she still had trouble putting weight on her left ankle.

Max gave me a quick kiss on the cheek when we walked inside, and he was off to meet his friends. Ashley and I stood just inside the entrance of the school. It was the closest she'd ever stood to me at school, the most she'd ever acknowledged having a sister, but I think she was afraid, literally, to show her face, for people to see her looking this way.

"It'll be okay." I nudged her, but she didn't respond. She just limped off toward her locker. I noticed that Austin wasn't waiting for her there; in fact, I didn't see him around anywhere, which was sort of odd. This was the first time all year that I'd seen Ashley at school by herself, Austin-free, and she looked like this whole different person all battered and bruised and alone. I almost felt a little sorry for her.

By lunchtime it had become very clear why Austin wasn't there. The whole school was buzzing with it, not just because Austin was popular but also because he was so good at baseball and the championships were coming up.

Max found me before lunch and whispered the news to me quickly on his way to class. Austin wasn't in school because Austin had caught mono.

It didn't take long for me to put two and two

together, that it was not Max the Nose had been in love with and making out with—it had been Austin all along.

And so the week that Ashley lost her beauty, her face, her glorious dance as queen of the spring formal, her chance to get to the Miss Arizona pageant, she also lost her boyfriend, her best friend, and—dare I say?—her dignity.

"Not bad," Ryan said to me in biology. "Mr. September made it all the way to April. If only we had known. Mr. April has kind of a nice ring to it, doesn't it?"

I smiled, even though it was horrible and mean, and deep down I felt sorry for Ashley. But as I thought about the eyes she shot at me when she acted like a know-it-all and insisted that the Nose had been making out with Max, I couldn't help it. "This is not her month, is it?" I hadn't really thought about it before I said it; it just sort of slipped out. Then I thought about the fact that April was the month our father had died, and it just seemed sort of unlucky and horrible all around.

Mrs. Connor had been telling us something about T. S. Eliot's interpretation of Keats yesterday, and she spouted off, "April is the cruelest month." She'd pulled her big, black floppy hat down dramatically over her eyes as she said it. We'd all looked at her sort of dumbly, waiting to see if she'd fallen off the deep end or something. "Oh never mind." She waved her hand in the air. "You're too young for my T. S. Eliot jokes. If you stick with it, maybe you'll read *The Waste Land* in twelfth-grade AP. That's the first line." She laughed. So not funny.

But just now that line popped into my head. I thought about the beautiful, cool starlit nights in the desert in April and the warm, sunny days, and the way that death had taken my father, and Ashley had been broken, and suddenly I worried that something terrible was about to befall me.

In English we moved on to Elizabeth Barrett Browning. As Mrs. Connor passed the day's poem down the rows she said, "Ah, Elizabeth and Robert. What an amazing love story." She was still wearing the black floppy hat that she'd had on yesterday, but today she'd lifted the flaps up so we could see her face, which I noticed looked even more illuminated than usual.

I stopped doodling in my notebook and looked over at the poem in front of me. "How do I love thee? Let me count the ways." Mrs. Connor shouted out the first line and jumped in front of the room. Her hat fell back down over her eyes. "I love thee to the depth and breadth and height my soul can reach."

"Oh"—Mrs. Connor sucked in her breath and closed her eyes—"imagine it, guys and gals: a love that consumes you so much that you can write something this stunning."

I wasn't sure I understood most of it. But I didn't think I loved Max to the depth and breadth and height my soul can reach, whatever the heck that meant.

"And here is something you should all know about Elizabeth," Mrs. Connor said. She was always doing this, trying to tell us something interesting about the poet, more than just the biographical stuff you would normally read in books. My father would've loved her. "The last word she ever uttered was the word *beautiful*. She was on her deathbed, and her husband, Robert, asked her how she was feeling. That's what she said in response: 'beautiful.'" She said the word softly, so it hung in the air for a minute before she said anything else.

I thought about my dad's last words to me, maybe to anyone, and I wondered what he would've said if I'd have asked him how he was feeling. *Beautiful* seemed like the perfect last thing to say, poetic even, and I wondered if she'd felt that way because her true love was sitting with her, if that's what real love did for you, made you feel beautiful in spite of everything.

Ashley had called my mother in the middle of the day to pick her up. She'd said her face and her ankle were killing her, and she couldn't concentrate, but I knew what it really was. She couldn't take the stares, the whispers. And really, I didn't blame her.

By the time I got home, she was already waiting for me in my bedroom. She was lying on my bed with a box of tissues, crying her eyes out. I was tempted to tell her to get up, to keep her gross mono germs to herself, in her own bed, but I just didn't have the heart, even though I resolved that I was going to switch my pillowcase before I went to sleep.

"I'm sorry," she said. "I'm such a bitch."

Ashley had never apologized to me before, for anything, so the only thing I could think to muster in response was, "Well, yeah. You sorta are."

"I shouldn't have said that to you about Max." She paused to blow her nose. "I mean some of the guys are like that, but not Max." She blew her nose again, and

I was wondering how she could be blowing so much since it was still broken, but I didn't ask. "Lexie just wanted you to think that Max didn't really like you, and I'm such an idiot. I went along with her."

I sat down next to her. A part of me wanted to kick her as hard as I could, and another part of me wanted to hug her. But I just sat there and did nothing.

"Max really likes you, you know. And he's a good guy. You're lucky, Melissa."

"Yeah." I shrugged. "I guess."

We sat there for a few minutes, until she said, in almost a whisper, "I was always so jealous of you."

"Me?" I didn't know what she would have to be jealous of when she was the one who was gorgeous and popular and an almost beauty queen.

"You can always just do your own thing, and you never care what anyone else thinks of you. You're so much like Dad."

"I am?" It wasn't fair that I'd been too young to remember him healthy, to really remember him, not just a few chance conversations and an evening of stargazing, but him, the person that he was, every single day.

"Yeah." She nodded. "Dad never followed anyone

else's rules. Mom used to yell at him for driving too fast and just doing what he pleased whenever he wanted to, even if no one else agreed with him. I remember when he got sick, he told me there was no way he was going to die. He just wasn't going to let himself. And he really believed that, even when Dr. Singh told him it wasn't true."

"I don't remember any of that," I said. "I wish I'd been older."

"I wish I could be more like him," she said.

"But you're you. You're beautiful."

"Not anymore."

"You will be again."

"But what does it matter?" She started crying again. "It'll be too late to do pageants, and all my friends will be laughing at me over this whole Austin thing."

"So." I shrugged. "You'll get new friends."

She laughed. "It's so easy for you. You're funny and smart, and what do I have?"

"You're funny and smart," I said, though I couldn't think of a single joke Ashley had ever cracked. "And besides, I'm totally going to fail biology," I said.

"Oh shut up. You are not."

I lay back so I was lying next to her and our

shoulders were touching. We both were staring at the ceiling, looking at the glow-in-the-dark stars that our dad had glued up there before he got sick, and I thought about that night I'd lain out on the grass with him and he'd told me that his favorite star was not the brightest. "Dad would've been really proud of you," I said.

She leaned her broken face on my shoulder, and the two of us just stayed there for a while, not saying another word.

The next night both Ashley and my mother helped me get ready for my date with Max. My mother curled my hair again, and Ashley picked out a really cute short-sleeved pink sweater from her closet for me to wear. Then she said she was going to lie down. "Are you all right?" my mother asked her. "You still don't seem like yourself, honey."

She shook her head.

"The pageant," I whispered, because I had just remembered. Tonight was the night. Ashley should've been downtown right now, taping her butt into her dress and layering foundation on her face, but instead she was here with us.

"Oh my goodness," my mother said. "That reminds

me." She ran into the kitchen, and then came back with an envelope, which she handed to Ashley. "Here," she said.

"What's this?" Ashley took the envelope and looked through it for a minute. Then she jumped up and squealed. "Ow," she said as she landed too hard on her ankle. "Ow." Then she squealed again and hugged my mother.

Ashley took the paper out of the envelope and waved it in my face. It was her entry into the premier set of pageants, which began with the first one in August, plenty of time for her to heal, to become beautiful all over again. It was the pageant circuit with the most scholarship money and the prettiest, most-elite girls, the one Ashley had always begged my mother to let her enter in the past.

"I thought you said this was too expensive?" Ashley said.

My mother shrugged. "I've picked up a few more clients lately at the salon, so we can swing it this year." She paused. "And besides, you deserve it, honey."

After I got all dressed and ready, I went into my room and stared at myself in the mirror. I was that other girl again, the pretty one with the made-up face and the bouncy, bouncy curls. I stood sideways and checked out my profile. In this sweater you couldn't even tell how small my boobs were, and the pink was soft and feminine and pretty.

I had butterflies in my stomach thinking about my date with Max, which was strange because we'd been spending time together all week. But I'd never been on a real date with a boy before, except for the dance, which wasn't really a real date, because he'd only sort of asked me at the last minute.

I heard a tapping at my window, and I jumped. *Not now, Ryan.* But I had no choice but to go and open the window for him anyway. He climbed in and looked at me, really looked at me. He stared long enough that I felt my face turning red. "What?" I finally said.

"Have you called her yet?"

I shook my head. I'd been so worried about everything with Max that I hadn't really been thinking about Sally.

He nodded. "I knew it."

"Why do you care so much anyway?" I paused. "I'm going to call her, all right?" And I was, at some point. It was funny how now that I knew exactly how and where to find her, I'd sort of lost my nerve to actually do it.

"Let's go right now. We can bike to her house."

"I have a date," I said.

"Oh." Maybe I imagined it, but I thought I saw his face drop, when I said the word *date*. It annoyed me, because he didn't have the right to do that, to judge or be angry or whatever, not after he'd ditched me for Courtney for months.

He stared at me for another moment and then started to say something but changed his mind.

"What?" I asked.

"Never mind."

"Say it."

He started to climb out the window, then stopped and turned back. "It's just, you look really nice. That's all." He jumped down and started running down the street toward his house.

The movie Max and I went to see was the action movie he'd been telling me about on the ride home the other day. I tried really hard to seem interested, but I just couldn't focus. Right away there was some big fight scene that just made me want to stop watching. And in my head I couldn't stop thinking about Ryan, about the way his face had looked as he'd looked at me, sort of surprised and thrilled all at the same time.

After about twenty minutes, Max reached over and put his arm around me, and then he leaned in and started kissing me. I kissed him back. He put his tongue in my mouth—not in this gentle, nice sort of way, but in this way where I felt like he was shoving it down my throat and I was going to have to cough. It was my first French kiss, and I hated it. Sort of slimy and aggressive, and I could not understand why people liked it.

I was trying to think of a polite way to get his tongue out of my mouth when I felt his hand inching toward my breast. I shifted a little to move his hand and hoped he'd get the hint. But he moved it right back. I squirmed a little more, and then he made a sudden move to put his hand under my shirt. I pulled away. "What's wrong?" he whispered. In the background, in the movie, there was a building exploding and people running and screaming, and it would've almost been something funny if it had been happening to someone else.

"Let's just watch the movie," I whispered back.

He laughed and started kissing me. And he put his hand right back under my shirt again, until I felt it on my stomach. His hand felt cold as it pressed against my skin just above my belly button. I reached my hand down and moved his hand out of my shirt again. But he put it right back. "Come on," I whispered. "Don't."

"Why not?" He kissed my ear and whispered, "I love that you're so new at this."

And then I knew it, absolutely, for sure. I didn't love him. Maybe I didn't even like him. So he was Max Healy. So every girl at school was in love with him. So what.

Maybe he wasn't trying to sleep with me just because I was a freshman, but still, it seemed like his idea of a date was feeling me up in the middle of an action movie. And if that's what a date with him was, then I was okay with not having any more, ever.

"Can you take me home?" I asked.

"What? Now? Are you kidding?" I shook my head, and he had this look of disbelief on his face, which then turned into a frown of annoyance.

"Never mind," I said. "I'll walk." I stood up and walked out of the movie theater, and I was sure that he wasn't going to follow me.

On the walk home I thought about what an idiot I'd been to think that I would've wanted a guy that every other girl wanted. If there was one thing I'd learned from my dad, it was to embrace the fact that I was different, that I wasn't like everyone else. "You're not a sheep," he used to say.

"What does that mean?"

"You don't follow the herd. You do your own thing."

And I always had, until this year. Until I met Courtney. Until Ryan ditched me. Until a part of me got so jealous that I just wanted to be beautiful and popular like Ashley because I thought that would solve everything. I thought about what Courtney had said when I'd told her about Max liking her in the beginning of the year. And she'd been right. All he'd wanted to do was get his hands up my shirt all along. Maybe it took a girl like Courtney to really understand a guy like Max.

I thought about Ryan's face as he'd stood in my room earlier in the night, and I knew I had to see him. Right now. As I got closer to my street, I started running. My feet were killing me in a pair of Ashley's sandals, but I didn't stop. I ran and I ran. And I ran.

When I got to Ryan's house, I was completely out of breath. I stood in his driveway for a second with my head between my knees, trying to keep my breath going. I wondered how fast my ribs were moving now.

His father's car was in the driveway, but I didn't see Ryan's bike parked in its normal spot, so I took a deep breath and rang the doorbell.

His father opened the door, and he was wearing his Border Patrol uniform, so I was guessing he'd just gotten home or he was just about to go out. He nodded at me. "Hello, Melissa. It's been a while." He had such a stern voice, and he was tall and looked very stately in his uniform. So the opposite of my father.

"Do you know where Ryan is?"

He nodded again. "He told me he went out to get something. For you, actually."

It hit me. Ryan had gone to find Sally by himself. My first reaction was to be angry, because what right did he have to find someone that was mine to find? But I wasn't all angry. This little part of me felt grateful that he cared enough to do it. Maybe this was his way of apologizing, after all. "Thank you." I waved and started running back toward my house.

I didn't go inside because I didn't want to explain to my mother or Ashley what had happened, and besides, I knew my mother would never let me get on my bike now, in the dark.

I pulled my bike out from the side of the house as quietly as I could, and I walked it down the street past my next-door neighbor's house. Then I hopped on and started riding.

The night was slightly cool, and the wind whipped through my hair, pulling the curls back behind my shoulders. It was a little harder than usual to pedal in Ashley's sandals, but I didn't care. Though I was riding toward Sally's house, it wasn't her I wanted to see.

This strange feeling came over me as I rode, this overwhelming sense of warmth and elation. All the anger I'd had for Ryan was gone. The world in which he'd ignored me and ditched me for Courtney felt very, very far away.

In its place there was this new world, one where he'd looked at me in my bedroom earlier in the evening in a way that no one else ever had looked at me before. And I absolutely knew it. Everyone had been right all along. I did want to be with him. Not just friends. I wanted him to look at me that way again. I wanted him to kiss me. I wanted to stand close enough to him to feel his breath on my face.

I pedaled so fast that my feet kept slipping off in clumsy motions that scraped the exposed skin. But I hardly even felt the scrapes, just the wind in my hair as I flew down the street. My heart was thudding against my chest and I was breathing heavily.

I am not exactly sure what happened next.

There was a horn that was so loud that it shocked me, and there was a crunch and a thud. I flew through the air with this unbelievable grace, like a humming-bird flittering on a bird of paradise.

And then there was darkness.

chapter *24*

There was a lot of darkness.

I heard noises in the background, but they were hard to really place. It was like being in that dream where there's something you know you really want, but you can't make yourself move to get it.

I saw people in my head, but they were foggy and blurred: Ryan, Ashley's broken face, my mother, my aunt Julie, even Courtney, some guy I didn't recognize, and a bright light like a halo. I kept thinking I should open my eyes. But I couldn't because I was tired. So very, very tired. Everything felt heavy and hard and long. And it just felt so good to sleep.

And then finally, I was able to open my eyes. The room was dark, and the furniture was sparse and shapeless against the black world. I had no idea where I was except there was a smell, the lemon Lysol scent and the vinegar that reminded me of Sunset Vistas and the hospital in Philadelphia. I was dead.

"Oh you're awake." This unfamiliar woman, whom I thought might be some sort of angel, was talking to me. Then I noticed her medical-center badge and her name tag. NURSE JUANITA DIAZ. I felt my ribs moving against my chest. I was breathing. I was alive. "I'll get your mother. Okay, hon?"

She walked back into the hallway, and I tried to remember how I got here, what happened. I remembered Ashley being thrown from a horse, and I wondered if I had been thrown from one too. Had I been riding Daffodil? But then, slowly, in pieces, it started to come back to me: my date with Max, riding my bike on the dark street, the horn, and the sickening thud.

My mother ran into the room and crushed me in a hug. "Oh, Melissa. Oh, sweetie, you gave me such a scare. What were you thinking?"

Ryan. But I didn't say it out loud.

Ashley stood behind her, and her face was still bruised

and hideous, so I knew I couldn't have been asleep for that long. "What happened?" I said.

"You got hit by a car, dumbass," Ashley said.

"Ashley, shush."

I couldn't help but smile because I knew that Ashley was jealous. I'd stolen her injury spotlight. "At least I didn't fall off a horse," I said.

"Girls." My mother reached down and pulled my hair out of my eyes—still curly. "Well, at least I know your brain's still working." She paused. "You have a concussion and a broken arm. They had to do surgery to set it. And you're going to be in a cast for six weeks."

I looked under the covers and was surprised to see she was right; there was a cast there. "It doesn't hurt."

"It will," she said. "I think they gave you something for the pain."

I noticed that I had an IV in my arm, and it reminded me instantly of my father in the hospice bed, in those last days, the morphine dripping down slowly into his arm.

"You were lucky," my mom said. "It could've been a lot worse." She kissed me on the head, then said, "I could just kill you for being so stupid." She paused. "You girls. Both of you. Sixteen years without a broken bone, and then all of this. All at once. It's too much." Tears sprang into her eyes, and she reached up quickly to wipe them away.

I knew she was right. I'd spent most of my life being worried about everything, every pain, every germ, that it might make me sick or kill me. For some reason I hadn't been thinking about it at all when I rode my bike on the pitch-dark streets. I'd been thinking about Ryan. Maybe that was love.

I leaned back against the pillow and closed my eyes. "What time is it?" I asked.

"Three A.M.," my mother said. Way too late to call Ryan. "Will you be okay if Ashley and I go home and get some rest?"

I nodded.

"We'll be back first thing in the morning." Ashley groaned, and my mother elbowed her. My mother leaned down and kissed me, and then they left me. In what might've been my deathbed.

I lay there awake for a while, just thinking about how lucky I was to be alive. I thought about the fact that it doesn't matter how much you wonder about things or worry about them. If they're going to happen to you, they will. According to Ashley, my dad really believed that his cancer wasn't going to kill him, but in the end there was nothing he could do to stop it. And somehow, I was hit by three thousand pounds of steel and I had only a broken arm and a concussion to show for it. Amazing.

I was discharged from the hospital around two o'clock the next afternoon, and though they were still giving me medication, my wrist started to ache and my head throbbed. I felt way worse than I did the night before, like I'd been hit by the proverbial bus, not a car.

Apparently the lady who'd hit me had run a red light, and the whole thing was her fault. This made my mother a little more angry at her and a little less angry at me, especially when she learned that the woman sent me flowers at the hospital. "The nerve," my mother said. "If she thinks she can just buy us off with some flowers."

"They're not even nice," Ashley sneered. "They're carnations, for godsakes."

"Well, I hope they throw the book at her," my mother said.

I felt a little bad because I knew that I hadn't really been watching, that I should've been paying more attention. "It was an accident," I said, so quietly that I wasn't sure if they heard me, because they both ignored my comment.

As soon as I got home, my mother set me up in bed with a tray of food, and I asked her to bring me the phone. "Don't talk too long," she said. "You need to rest."

I nodded and didn't tell her that I planned on telling Ryan to come over.

I called him, and I felt my heart beating faster. A broken arm and a concussion had done little to dull the excitement I'd felt last night as I'd raced toward him on my bike.

He picked up. "Come over," I said. "Come in through my window." I hung up without giving him a chance to answer.

Ten minutes later there was tapping. I pulled off the tray with one arm, struggled to stand, and limped toward the window.

"Jesus, Mel. What happened?" He reached up and touched the lump the size of a golf ball on my forehead.

"Ow." I hadn't known how tender it was before he touched it.

"You go on one date, and you look like this?"

I laughed. "I left in the middle of the movie, and then I came to look for you."

"I know," he said. "My dad told me." He paused. "I was in the wash."

"You were?" I shook my head, so I'd been riding in the wrong direction, all for nothing. I wondered what would've happened if I'd ended up at Sally's house, and I wondered if the car that hit me was some kind of divine intervention, keeping me from ever getting there. Like God reaching his hand down or something and telling me not to find her. "Your dad said you went to find something for me."

He nodded. "I did. I wanted it to be a surprise." He paused. "I was looking in the wash for more glass, you know, from the same piece."

I nodded. "I thought you'd gone to look for Sally," I whispered.

"I wanted to make you something. I don't know, a memorial or something for your dad."

I started to cry, and I couldn't stop the tears, even though they hurt my head.

"We can still go look for her together if you want."

I shook my head. I wanted to tell him that wasn't why I was crying, that I wasn't sure I wanted to find Sally anymore, because maybe it didn't even matter who she was. Maybe it was better remembering things the way I remembered them. Maybe I didn't want to know anything else, anything that might tarnish the memories and make my dad into some other person that I never really even knew at all.

Ryan put his thumbs on my cheeks and wiped away my tears. We stood there like that for a moment, my tears falling over his thumbs, the two of us staring into each other's eyes. There was so much to say, and no way for me to possibly say it all and get it right.

So, without saying anything, without thinking it through, I stretched up and kissed him.

I kissed him softly, on the mouth, and I knew he was surprised because he didn't move for a second. But then he kissed me back.

I wasn't thinking about my concussion or my broken arm, or the fact that I hadn't taken a shower since before I'd been hit by a car, flung in the dirty street, carried in an ambulance and operated on. I wasn't thinking at all. Just feeling. His lips were warm, and when I kissed him, I felt this warmth in my chest, this energy that wanted to burst right out of me. And this feeling, this overwhelming electric sensation that he was the person I wanted to be with.

He pulled back. "What about Max?" he whispered.

I shrugged. "What about him?"

"I thought you liked him."

I shook my head. "No." I paused. "I think I just thought I should, you know?"

He touched my cast softly. "Aren't you even going to tell me what happened?"

I didn't want to, because I felt embarrassed and enormously stupid. But I blurted it all out anyway, leaving out the details about exactly why I'd left Max in the movie theater.

Ryan pulled me into a hug, and I put my head against his chest. His heart beat loud and strong in my ear, and for once his breath sounded even, not wheezy at all. "How are you feeling now?" he whispered into my hair.

"Beautiful," I whispered back.

It was like it was something I'd always known but hadn't known how to say until right that very moment.

chapter *25*

It was a little surreal going back to school after my accident, being Ryan's girlfriend and all, and having people know who I was. Somehow this rumor got started that Max and I had gotten in a fight on our date, he'd left me by the side of the road, and then I'd gotten hit by the car. I'm not sure where the rumor began, but I suspected Ashley.

I didn't correct people, and there was this part of me that enjoyed it. Girls I didn't even know, who were juniors and seniors even, smiled at me in the hallways and asked me about my arm. I told them, always, that it could've been much worse, which, of course, was also the truth.

But don't worry about Max—two weeks after our date he started dating a cheerleader named Amy, who is beautiful and red-haired and bouncy, and who, Ashley told me for a fact, really does have fake boobs.

Ashley had been wrong about being laughed at by her friends, because it seemed like all the popular girls had taken Ashley's side against the Nose. I noticed that the Nose no longer sat at the cool table at lunch. She'd moved to a table by the back window and pretended to study, and the strange thing was, even when Austin finally came back to school, I never saw the two of them together. Whenever I saw Austin, he was hanging around with the other guys on the team, high-fiving in the hall-way and hollering by the bank of lockers. And Ashley was always with "Bobblehead" Beth the cheerleader, who'd moved into the spot of her new best friend.

At home it was Ashley, not me, who told my mother that Ryan and I were now a couple. "Oh?" My mother turned to me. "What about Max?"

"She and Ryan totally make a cute couple," Ashley said, ignoring my mother's question about Max. "Every-one thinks so."

I felt my face turning red and hot, because I still wasn't used to it, the way being someone's girlfriend made your feelings about him so loud and out in the open.

"Well, I always thought he was a nice boy," my mother said, but she wouldn't look at me, and I couldn't shake the feeling that she was angry.

It wasn't her fault that she knew nothing about my terrible date with Max. She'd asked me over and over again what had happened that night, but all I'd told her was that I'd needed some air, that that's why I'd gotten on the bike.

"It was stupid, Melissa." She'd said it probably a dozen times already. "Riding your bike at night. You're smarter than that. You could've gotten yourself killed."

"I know," I told her. And I promised never ever to do it again. A promise I intended to keep.

Still, she refused to buy me another bike. "You'll walk," she said, "and drive at some point." Why she thought this would be any less dangerous didn't make complete sense, but I could kind of see her point about the bike.

I got my cast off the Friday before finals week. My mother took the afternoon off, and she picked me up from school at noon.

"I can't wait to get this thing off," I said as I got into the car. The cast felt like a weight and the skin underneath it had been itching terribly for the past few weeks. At the same time I was nervous because the doctor had already told us that there would be a scar from the surgery. And I wasn't sure what to expect, how hideous and deformed it might make me look.

My mother nodded, but she kept her eyes on the road, straight ahead of her. At the end of the street she took a right instead of the left she should've taken to head toward the doctor's office. "Where are you going?" I asked.

She didn't answer. Then she made another right. And I knew exactly where she was headed. She drove slowly down the same street I'd pedaled with ferocious speed the night I'd been searching for Ryan, for Sally.

And then suddenly, she pulled off to the side of the road and parked up on the sidewalk, right there, right at the spot I'd been hit.

"I just want to know," she said, "what you were doing here." Her eyes were still on the road, not on me.

"I told you," I said quietly. "I needed some air."

She cleared her throat. "I have the rest of the day

off from work, so I've got time." She looked down at her watch. "And your doctor's appointment is in thirty minutes. It would be a shame to miss it and have to reschedule." She turned off the car and took the key out of the ignition.

"You're blackmailing me?" I was more surprised than anything, not only that she was threatening to make me stay in the dreadful fiberglass for another few days, but also that she cared so much.

She turned and looked right at me. "Sweetie," she said, "I . . ." She paused. "Your sister always talks to me, but you . . ." She shrugged. "I don't know how to get through to you."

It was a combination of feeling bad for her and really just wanting to get my cast off, but I took a deep breath and let the story pour right out of me. All of it: what Grandma Harry had said about Sally Bedford, searching for her with Ryan at Charles and Large, pedaling toward her house the night of the accident, and then finally, my new resolve to stop looking for her, my thought that the accident had been a sign.

When I was done talking, she was silent for a minute, and then she said, "Thank you for telling me the truth."

She put the key back in the ignition and drove to the doctor's office without saying another word.

Later that night I was lying on my bed attempting to learn the biology flash cards Ryan had made me so I could study for the final. My arm still felt limp, and the skin looked flaky and surreal. The scar was smaller than I thought it would be, but it was still pretty red and ugly-looking. I kept getting distracted and staring at it and thinking about the fact that it would be there forever. The doctor had said that it would fade over time, but still, I knew that every time I'd look down at my wrist, I'd have a reminder of the night I could've died.

My mother knocked at the door, then opened it before I had a chance to respond. "How's your arm?" she asked. I noticed she was holding a medium-sized clear plastic box.

"Okay." I wondered if she was still mad, if she was coming in to tell me I was grounded.

"Here." She thrust the box at me.

"What's this?"

"Some of your dad's things, from high school. I still had them put away from when I helped Grandma Harry move out of her house." I was surprised because I hadn't known she'd kept anything of his other than that one picture from Sears. But I took the box.

"Why are you giving me this?" I asked.

She sat down on the edge of my bed. "Sweetie," she said, "anytime you want to know something about your dad, all you have to do is ask." She paused. "Everything you'd want to know about Sally Bedford is in here." She leaned in and gave me a hug. Then she whispered in my ear, "I still miss him too, you know."

After she left, I stared at the box, trying to decide whether or not to open it. Maybe the accident hadn't been a sign of anything, I reasoned. Maybe it had just been the dark and two people who weren't paying attention. Nothing more.

Everything I wanted to know was sitting right in front of me, and I couldn't let it go. I wanted to know the truth, so I took a deep breath and lifted the lid.

The contents of the box: a high-school yearbook, five letters, four pictures, a playbill for *Guys and Dolls*, and a box of clarinet reeds. An odd assortment of objects that seemed to sum up my dad's high-school years and maybe the kind of person he was in general, an interesting combination of thinker and dreamer.

I flipped through the yearbook first, slowly. In his senior picture my dad appeared nothing like I remembered him, so young and handsome, and he had this look on his face that reminded me of the way Ashley looked at school, very important and in charge. I learned my father had been a part of the pep band, the debate club, the National Honor Society, and the drama club. And there, right along with him in both debate and drama, was Sally Bedford.

She was thinner and younger-looking in these pictures than in the one I'd found on the internet, and she had a much cuter bob cut and smile here.

And then when I flipped toward the back of the book, there was a picture of her and my dad. They were sitting on a wall together. She was leaning into him with her head on his shoulder. He had his arm around her, and he looked as if he was laughing, as if there was this sense of joy bursting right out of him that he just couldn't contain.

I traced my finger over his face and then over hers. And for some reason I thought about me and Ryan, about holding his hand as we walked up the steps to our school the first time as a couple, about the intense way my body had felt alive and the way everything else had faded, become background noise. Maybe that's what

Sally Bedford had done for my father.

There were also a few loose pictures of them at what looked like two different formal dances. Sally wore a red puffy-sleeved dress and hung on tightly to my father, who had on a tux with a matching red cummerbund. In another picture they matched in an emerald green.

I flipped through the yearbook a little more and read what Sally wrote to my father, and then I read the letters. When I was done, I put everything back into the box and put the lid back on, and then I went and sat at my desk with my journal, picked up a pen, and started writing, until the real and the imagined blurred together into something that was part truth, part fantasy, but all the same felt like an answer.

Sally Bedford and Tom McAllister

The first time Tom McAllister saw Sally Bedford, it was the first day of his junior year. She was sitting under a paloverde tree eating her lunch. Everyone else gathered on the school grounds in clumps, but not Sally. She was new to school, and she was sitting all alone. She looked up and caught him watching her, and she gave a little wave. He waved back, though he felt his face turning red, knowing he'd been caught staring.

He saw her again later that week at the first meeting

of the debate club, and then later that month at the tryouts for Guys and Dolls. *Each time she gave a little wave, and he nodded. Tom had no time for girls. He was worrying about his SATs and his grades and having enough diverse activities to get into a good college, with a scholarship.*

Sally was a senior and a very talented singer and a dancer. She won the part of Miss Adelaide, the female lead. Tom had only joined drama because his mother thought it would look good on his college applications, and he landed a part in the chorus. He suspected that it was only because everyone who tried out was guaranteed a part, because the director asked him not to sing louder than a whisper.

Sally was small and a little mousy, shy and a little wilted like a flower in the Arizona summer sun. But onstage she was brilliant. Amazing. Tom watched her sing from the back of the stage, and her voice, clear and bright like wind chimes, gave him chills.

One day when her understudy was practicing, she came and sat next to him. "You're always watching me," she said. "Why?"

"I'm not," Tom lied. He cleared his throat. "You're very special." He knew how weird it sounded as soon as it came it. "I mean talented," he said. Yes, that had been what he'd meant, hadn't it?

"Thank you," she said. She stood up. "Are you busy this weekend?"

He wasn't.

They went to see a movie. She drove because she had her own car and he didn't. "I don't know what kind of girl picks you up," his mother said, shaking her head.

"The kind of girl who has a car."

At the end of the night she pulled up in front of his house. She turned off the car. They stared at each other. Silence. They stared some more. Finally, he said, "Where did you learn to sing like that?"

She laughed, and she leaned in and kissed him.

For a year they were inseparable. Every weekend she drove them out on dates. They became debate partners. He helped her rehearse her lines. They went to the fall formal and the prom. They spent the summer at the community pool under the lofty shade of the cabana.

In August she left to go to college. "We'll still stay together," she said tearfully. "I'll come home every weekend. I'll write you every day."

When she left, he felt like a part of him had been chipped away, like there was this empty, burning pit in his stomach—or at least that's what he wrote in a letter he never sent her.

She called a few times, but after two weeks her calls stopped. She'd promised to come home for Labor Day weekend, but she didn't show.

Tom spent the weekend in his bedroom with his blinds closed. "You can't just lie in here and mope," his mother said, trying to rustle him out of bed.

"I can," he said, "and I will."

And then she sent him a letter, A Dear Tom, This-is-never-going-to-work letter.

He went back to his bedroom every day after school, every weekend. He couldn't imagine his life without her. He suddenly understood what it meant to have a broken heart, because his hurt, and it was hard for him to breathe without feeling like he was suffocating (at least that's what he wrote in another letter he never sent). His mother told him there would be other girls, but he just shook his head.

He dropped out of drama and debate club. He let his mother fill out his college applications for him, but he was no longer interested in Stanford. He thought if he went to the same school as she did, he would find her and win her back. His mother, secretly, did not send this application in.

Life went on. He got into other colleges. He met his real soul mate, Cynthia. He got a job, got married, had children.

And then he got sick.

And in the in between, he and Sally ended up working
at the same place. Maybe they talked again. Maybe she apolo-
gized. Maybe she asked for help with her taxes. Maybe they
had lunch and laughed about old times.

Or maybe they didn't.

I put my pencil down. This next part I didn't know, but suddenly it didn't seem to matter what else had happened. I was sure that when Grandma Harry had mentioned Sally, mentioned the terrible thing she'd done, that she was talking about the girl who had broken my father's heart in high school, not the woman he may have talked to again all these years later.

And that was absolutely all I needed to know. All I wanted to know.

chapter *26*

And then it was summer again.

Somehow, I survived my freshman year, passed biology with the help of Ryan, and even finished with an A in English, poetry and all.

In June Ashley got her new permanent teeth put in, and they are perfect-looking and even whiter and shinier than her real ones. Once her nose was fixed up, she admitted that she liked it better than the old one. It was sort of like she got the nose job she always wanted. For free.

She was training for the premier pageant circuit my mother had signed her up for, and my mother even convinced her to join a gym to get into shape rather than resort to living on carrot sticks.

For about a month after school ended, we actually got along. We slept late in the mornings, and then we got up and watched *All My Children* together while we were still in our pj's. We lounged around on the couch like two bums, and we talked trash about all the soap-opera actresses and who looked fat and who didn't.

And then one day, in the middle of June, Austin stopped by. He and Ashley went to sit out on the back porch and talk. I tried to watch out the window of the family room, but I had no idea what they were saying. They looked serious and calm and not mad at each other. After a few minutes they both stood up, and they hugged.

Austin left out the back, and she walked back in. Her face was bright red from sitting in the heat, and she went to get a glass of water. "What did *he* want?" I asked.

She shrugged. "He wanted to get back together with me."

"Seriously?" I said. "You could have any guy you want."

"I know," she said. "That's why I told him I just wanted to be friends."

She smiled, and I felt a little triumphant for her.

A few weeks later Ashley met a new guy at the gym. He was a tennis player and a sophomore in college—something she didn't tell my mother, but I overheard her tell Bobblehead on the phone.

It didn't take her long to ditch *All My Children* for scanning ESPN for tennis matches, and I decided if there was one sport more boring to watch than baseball, it was tennis. But for some reason I sat with her and watched it anyway.

By the beginning of July, Kevin had stopped sending my mother flowers. It was something we'd all gotten used to, the weekly FTD delivery. But we also knew it couldn't last forever.

"What, no flowers today?" my mother said when she got home from work. Ashley and I shook our heads, and my mother looked a little sad.

"You should call him," I finally said.

My mother cocked her head to the side and put her hand on her hip. "You don't even like him."

"He's okay," I said.

"You should," Ashley chimed in quietly. Maybe it was because she liked her new face even better than the old one that she forgave him, because it wasn't like Ashley to be the bigger person.

"No, I can't," my mother said. "It's been too long." She paused. "Hasn't it?"

I shrugged. Ashley shook her head.

My mother pulled us both into a hug and said, "Oh, my girls. You're both getting so grown up, aren't you?" She paused. "Ashley, one more year and you'll be off to college, and then before I know it, Melissa, you'll leave me too."

Ashley walked into the family room, grabbed the cordless phone, and handed it to my mother.

Ryan and I can no longer ride our bikes in the wash, since I am still without a bike. But still, at night, after my mom and Ashley go to sleep, I climb out my bedroom window, jump down into the crushed rock and the garden of purple lantana my mother is working on, and walk down to Ryan's house. Sometimes we hang out in his backyard and watch the stars. One night, as we are lying on the small patch of grass, I tell him the truth about Sally, how my father had dated her in high school, and then when she went away to college, how she left him, just like that.

Ryan squeezes my hand. "That's never going to

happen to us," he whispers.

"No," I agree. "It won't."

Then, when the summer rains come, in the beginning of July, we walk to the edge of the wash and watch the river run through it, rough and terrible and almost like rapids.

Just before the end of July, when we know the water will soon disappear and the wash will be ours again to ride (or walk) and scavenge as we please, Ryan tells me that he has an idea. "Bring your glass tomorrow night," he says. So I do.

We stand there on the edge of the temporary river, and it feels like the edge of the world. "How long did you say this glass would last again?" he asks.

"A million years," I say. Now that it's been so long, it's a struggle to remember my dad's voice, exactly what it sounded like. But I think I can still remember how it sounded when he said that. A million years. The way he stretched it into something stunning, so much longer than any of us could imagine.

"At the count of three, let's throw them in," he says. "Let's let the water carry them."

I hesitate for a moment. "I don't know if I'm ready," I say.

Ryan takes my hand, the one that is not holding the piece of glass. "You are," he says.

He counts. One. Two. Three.

I hold my hand out and let go, and I watch the glass fly through the air and land with a small, graceful plop in the water, like a tiny stone.

I wonder where it will end up, who else might find it. And how it might journey on and on and on for what feels like forever.

Ryan puts his arm around me, and we stand there and enjoy the water for a while because, before we know it, it will be gone.

acknowledgments

My deepest thanks to my editors, Jill Santopolo, whose overwhelming support made writing this book a dream come true for me, and whose kind and smart suggestions always make my stories shine brighter, and Ruta Rimas, who nurtured this book through to publication and whose enthusiasm and support have been nothing short of amazing. Thank you to Alessandra Balzer and Donna Bray for graciously taking me in and giving this book a home. And an enormous thanks to everyone else at HarperCollins who has worked so diligently on my behalf.

I owe a debt of gratitude to my agent, Jessica Regel,

without whom, I am entirely sure, this book never would have existed. Thank you for your always sage advice and your tireless support. I am also grateful to everyone else at the Jean V. Naggar Literary Agency who works on my behalf—I feel so honored to be a part of your amazing group of authors.

A big thanks to Sarah Shealy and Barbara Fisch at Blue Slip Media for all the work they did in getting the word out about this book. You two are a publicity dream come true!

Thank you to my wonderful parents and sister, Alan, Ronna, and Rachel Cantor, always an incredible source of love and support in everything I do, and writing this book was no exception.

Thank you to my children and to my husband, Gregg Goldner, not only for giving me the time I needed to write this book but also for making my world an infinitely better place. And for being my relentless promoter and web designer, Gregg, I can't thank you enough!

And to my loved ones who have suffered from cancer, you were in my head and my heart as Melissa's story came to life.